*Fox in plain Sight* is a work of fiction. Names, characters, places, and incidents are the products of the author's imagination and are used fictitiously. Any resemblance to actual events, locales, or persons, living or dead, is entirely coincidental.
This book was previously published under the title Seek as part of the Phoenix Code series.

Published in the United States

Cover design: Leah Kaye Suttle
Author Photo: © Marti Corn Photography

Printed in the United States of America

# Books by Tina Folsom

Ace on the Run (Code Name Stargate, Book 1)
Fox in plain Sight (Code Name Stargate, Book 2)
Time Quest: Reversal of Fate
Samson's Lovely Mortal (Scanguards Vampires, Book 1)
Amaury's Hellion (Scanguards Vampires, Book 2)
Gabriel's Mate (Scanguards Vampires, Book 3)
Yvette's Haven (Scanguards Vampires, Book 4)
Zane's Redemption (Scanguards Vampires, Book 5)
Quinn's Undying Rose (Scanguards Vampires, Book 6)
Oliver's Hunger (Scanguards Vampires, Book 7)
Thomas's Choice (Scanguards Vampires, Book 8)
Silent Bite (Scanguards Vampires, Book 8 1/2)
Cain's Identity (Scanguards Vampires, Book 9)
Luther's Return (Scanguards Vampires, Book 10)
Blake's Pursuit (Scanguards Vampires, Book 11)
Fateful Reunion (Scanguards Vampires, Book 11 1/2)
John's Yearning (Scanguards Vampires, Book 12)
Lover Uncloaked (Stealth Guardians, Book 1)
Master Unchained (Stealth Guardians, Book 2)
Warrior Unraveled (Stealth Guardians, Book 3)
Guardian Undone (Stealth Guardians, Book 4)
Immortal Unveiled (Stealth Guardians, Book 5)
Protector Unmatched (Stealth Guardians, Book 6)
Demon Unleashed (Stealth Guardians, Book 7)
A Touch of Greek (Out of Olympus, Book 1)
A Scent of Greek (Out of Olympus, Book 2)
A Taste of Greek (Out of Olympus, Book 3)
A Hush of Greek (Out of Olympus, Book 4)
Teasing (The Hamptons Bachelor Club, Book 1)
Enticing (The Hamptons Bachelor Club, Book 2)
Beguiling (The Hamptons Bachelor Club, Book 3)
Scorching (The Hamptons Bachelor Club, Book 4)
Alluring (The Hamptons Bachelor Club, Book 5)
Sizzling (The Hamptons Bachelor Club, Book 6)

# Fox in plain Sight

Code Name Stargate – Book 2

# TINA FOLSOM

# 1

"Gotcha!"

Nick Young pumped his fist in the air and let out a triumphant growl while continuing to stare into the computer screen. A red dot was blinking on a map of Washington, D.C. Next to it, an IP address flashed.

"You bastard! Did you really think you could outwit me? Looks like I'm smarter than you after all."

The guy had made a tiny mistake, whether out of stupidity or laziness, Nick didn't know, nor did he care. What counted was that now Nick knew where to find him.

He felt a genuine smile curve his lips, the first in a long time. For over a month now, he'd been playing cat-and-mouse with an online adversary who was trying to keep him out of the servers that held crucial data Nick had been looking for ever since the secret CIA program he'd been part of had been compromised three years earlier.

Nick memorized the address the dot was pointing to and logged off. He flipped the lid of his laptop shut and stashed it in his backpack. Then he pulled an old keyboard out of the drawer, hooked it up to the dinosaur PC that he kept as a decoy and connected a mouse to it.

Should anybody find him and try to trace what he'd been doing, the files he'd planted on the hard drive of the old desktop he'd bought second-hand would lead any pursuer on a wild goose chase. With a little luck, nobody would be looking for a second computer, and he'd be long gone before they were on his tail and could kill him like they'd killed Henry Sheppard, his mentor and the leader of the Stargate program.

The same fate was waiting for him and his fellow operatives—CIA agents selected not for their physical abilities but their unique mental skills. Each of the Stargate agents, including Henry Sheppard, possessed the gift of premonition. Three years ago, somebody had decided that the Stargate agents presented a danger and killed the leader of the program.

When Nick had received Sheppard's mental call, his world had collapsed.

*"Stargate down."*

He could still hear the alert echo in his mind. He'd left everything behind and gone into hiding. But the need to know what had happened to Sheppard and the other agents had driven him back to Washington D.C. Back into the lion's den.

"Keep your friends close and your enemies closer," Nick murmured to himself now. It had become his mantra since Sheppard's death.

It had been easy to create a new identity. His skills as a hacker had proven to be invaluable. His new identity was ordinary. No family, no special skills, a low profile all around. He kept himself afloat by creating websites for small businesses around the world.

He lived in an apartment in a run-down house the absentee landlord was renting to him for cash so he wouldn't have to tax the proceeds. Every month, Nick deposited the money in a mailbox. Fine with him. He wasn't exactly keen on the government right now.

He'd served his country as a CIA agent for many years, and they'd failed to protect him and his colleagues. He was on his own now, responsible for his own life, and out for revenge. One day, he'd make sure the men who'd killed Sheppard would pay for what they'd done.

And the person at the other end of the IP address he'd traced would help him find the responsible party. Whether he wanted to or not.

Nick knew of many ways to persuade another person to do whatever he wanted him to do. His favorite toy to elicit such cooperation was his Glock. The cold metal never failed to convince the other party that loyalty was overrated and life was a fleeting thing.

At first sight, people always assumed that Nick was merely a computer geek and not to be feared. Maybe his boy-next-door looks and his quiet demeanor were responsible for that misperception. But those people who cared to give him a more thorough look would discover what he really was: a man who knew how to handle himself and the weapons at his disposal. Sheppard had made sure of that. All the men he'd selected for his Stargate program had to undergo rigorous training at The Farm, just like all other CIA agents, though it wasn't necessary for their ultimate work. But maybe Sheppard had known all along that one day his protégés would have to rely on those very skills to survive.

Nick inspected his gun, pulled the magazine from it, and made sure it was fully loaded, before reinserting it. Then he stashed it in the secret, padded compartment in his backpack. Lifting his foot onto the chair, he pulled up one pant leg and slid a knife into the hidden pocket in his boot. Sometimes a little knife was all he needed to come to an agreement with an adversary. It was less conspicuous than a gun, and much less noisy should he need to use it.

There wasn't much else to do. Nick let his gaze wander around the room. The shredder bin was empty. The few pieces of mail he received were solicitations addressed to *current resident*. Any mail related to his website business went to a P.O. box, anything related to any bank accounts he received in electronic form. Only the utility bills came to the house, and those he paid promptly and then shredded. For all intents and purposes, Nick Young didn't exist. But Fox was still alive. It had been his code name while in the Stargate program. And the few other Stargate members he'd met—since Sheppard had always insisted on keeping them apart as much as possible—only knew him by that name.

He'd been proud when his mentor had given him the name. It showed that Sheppard understood him. Because Nick *was* like a fox, cunning and clever. And he would need these skills now to ferret out the computer genius who'd been fighting him online. Now Fox would bring the fight to his doorstep and up the stakes.

Showtime.

# 2

A parking garage? Really? How *Deep Throat* could this guy get?

Michelle Andrews shivered despite the fact that it was sweltering hot in D.C. Her tank top and short skirt had been just fine at the coffee shop where she'd spent the morning, but the massive concrete walls, floors, and ceilings of the dark underground garage kept the air surprisingly cold.

She hadn't expected this meeting. When she'd received the text message on her burner phone, she'd panicked. It was the reason she'd spilled coffee on the table and rushed to the barista to ask for a rag to clean it up. Unfortunately, those few seconds of inattentiveness had caused her to disconnect much later than planned from the online trace she'd been running.

She replayed the incident in her mind once more. Was there any chance that the hacker she'd been trying to get a lock on had instead gotten the drop on her? Michelle shook her head. No. Nobody was better than her. Since she hadn't been able to catch him, he wouldn't have had enough time to catch her either. She'd taken ample precautions to remain hidden. Still, with all that had happened in her life lately, she was on edge and had started doubting herself and her abilities.

Nervously, she twisted her pendant between her fingers, an old habit that died hard. The little memento from her time as a member of Anonymous, the worldwide hacker cooperative, always lent her strength—and reminded her of what had gotten her into this mess in the first place.

Nevertheless, she would get through this, no matter what the shady *Deep Throat* character who'd requested this meeting threw at her now. Whether he was FBI, CIA, or NSA, she didn't know. Nor did it really matter. Any of those government agencies had sufficient powers to lock her up for the rest of her life if she didn't do their bidding. They held all the cards. She held none. She'd become a pawn in whatever game they were playing and would have to play along until she found a way out.

When she heard footsteps echo against the bare concrete walls, she made a motion to turn.

"You know the drill," her handler said.

Michelle froze, facing away from him. "Mr. Smith." It wasn't his real name. When he'd first contacted her and she'd asked him who he was, he'd paused for a long while before saying, "How about Smith? Does that sound good to you?"

She'd never seen his face, though from his accent and speech pattern she assumed he was well-educated and middle-aged. There was a nasal quality to his voice that made her picture him as a short, balding guy with a beer belly and pale skin. Of course, she could be completely wrong, but didn't everybody like to picture their enemies as ugly and unattractive?

"I'm very disappointed in you, Miss Andrews."

Instinctively, she pulled up her shoulders, tensing.

"You've had a month now, and what have you got to show for yourself? Nothing. My employers are not very happy with you." He sighed. "And neither am I."

She contemplated his words and chose her own with care. "I've done what you've asked me to." *Asked* was not exactly the right word. *Coerced* was more like it.

"Really, Miss Andrews? I have the feeling you haven't given it your all yet. Or do I need to remind you of what will happen if you don't comply?"

She needed no reminder. "Mr. Smith, I've used my skills—"

"When we caught you," he interrupted, his voice sharp and cold, "your skills seemed to be much more refined. I find it odd that you can't get a trace on a hacker when you yourself were immersed in that community for so long."

"It would help if I knew what this guy is after, so I don't have to keep wasting my time on hackers that you're not interested in."

A low growl came from behind her, and she realized that he'd come closer without her noticing. A cold chill raced down her spine and made her blood freeze in her veins.

"You know too much already, Miss Andrews." He inhaled. "It's dangerous to know too much. Haven't you learned anything?"

She shivered, her palms beading with sweat.

"You were a very bad girl. Do you remember?"

Michelle didn't answer, knowing he didn't expect her to.

"Hacking into servers you had no business being in. And your friends at Anonymous, they couldn't help you either, could they? Because now that we have you, nobody can help you. You work for us now, or you'll go to prison. It would be a shame. A pretty girl like you. You know what they do with somebody like you in prison?"

She didn't want to know. "I'm doing what you've asked me to do."

"Do it faster. I'm getting impatient. How hard can it be to find a hacker who's been trying to get into our servers, hmm? Aren't you the best? Or was that a lie?"

"I am the best," Michelle insisted, not because she was arrogant, but because admitting that she wasn't would surely get her killed.

"Good, then prove it. Give me something I can work with. You want to keep your freedom, don't you?"

She nodded automatically.

"The hacker in exchange for your freedom. You know I'm not bluffing. Tell me you understand."

"I understand."

"Good, then here's what you do: find him, but don't spook him. If he finds out that you're onto him, he's gone. Do you get that? You have ten days. If you can't deliver him by then, our deal is off, and you'll be prosecuted. Not as an American, but as a terrorist. You should have thought twice about what you were getting yourself into when you hacked into the Department of Defense's servers. You committed an act of terrorism." He clicked his tongue. "Very despicable indeed."

"I never—"

His hand on her shoulder made her swallow her words. The urge to turn around to look into the face of her tormentor was strong, but she suppressed it, knowing it would earn her a bullet in the head.

"No more excuses."

Her heart raced, and her pulse thundered in her ears. Rage made her clench her teeth. She wasn't a terrorist, far from it. She and her fellow hackers at Anonymous had been trying to uncover documents about the United States' involvement in the latest Middle East conflict and the real reasons behind their support for a regime that tortured its own citizens. She'd wanted the American public to know the truth. That wasn't terrorism. It was freedom of speech. She hadn't hurt anybody by hacking into government servers.

Nevertheless, she was paying for it now. They'd tried to get her to give up the other members of Anonymous who'd taken part in this project, but she'd refused. She was no snitch. Besides, Michelle hardly knew who the others were, only knew them by their screen names.

The sudden silence made her pause in her thoughts. She listened intently, but there was nothing. Not even the sound of breathing.

"Mr. Smith?"

There was no reply. Michelle spun around. She was alone in the dark underground parking garage. Alone, except for a few parked cars.

Clutching her messenger bag that held her laptop, she walked toward the elevator. Ten days was all she had left. Judging by the little she'd accomplished in the previous four weeks, she had a snowball's chance in hell of delivering the elusive hacker Smith was looking for. Without any clue as to what the person was actually after, she couldn't narrow down her search. Did Smith have any idea how many hackers attacked governmental servers every single day? Despite that obstacle she'd come across one particular individual who'd piqued her interest, but she hadn't been able to get a lock on him yet.

Essentially, she was looking for a needle in a haystack. A needle she couldn't afford to search for any longer, because if she didn't get away before the ten days were up, she'd be as good as dead.

It was time to plan her escape while continuing to pretend that she was following Smith's request, so he wouldn't catch on to her deception until it was too late.

# 3

This wasn't going to be quite as easy as he'd thought at first.

For starters, the IP address Nick had traced had led him to the Foggy Bottom neighborhood of D.C., an area that not only housed George Washington University, but also the George Washington Medical Center and numerous government buildings ranging from the World Bank and the International Monetary Fund to the Federal Reserve Building and the Department of the Interior.

In addition, the address wasn't a private home, or even an office. It was a coffee shop with free WiFi access. Anybody with a laptop could hook into the coffee shop's free internet and be on their IP address. An extremely odd choice for the computer genius with whom Nick had been at odds during the last few weeks. Why would somebody risk working on an open internet connection where others might be able to listen in? Or was it pure genius, hiding in plain sight?

Nick glanced around the coffee shop. At least two dozen students, young doctors, and suits were hunched over their laptops, working, surfing, and reading. At first glance, none of them looked like a hacker, but then, what exactly did a hacker look like? He knew that appearances could be deceptive.

Was he the scruffy student, who was balancing his laptop on his knees while eating a muffin with one hand? Or the young woman in the white doctor's coat and the dark circles under her eyes, eyes that kept falling shut while she stared intensely into her computer monitor? Maybe the heavy-set black guy in the gray suit was the man in question, trying to divert any suspicion by looking all businesslike with his manicured nails and trendy haircut.

In short, it could be anybody.

This would take some time. He might as well get comfortable and find a corner from which to watch the comings and goings. Sooner or later, his CIA training would kick in, and he'd pick up on the tells his suspect was giving off. He'd learned that nobody could hide his true nature forever. Particularly once they relaxed and let down their guard, their true self emerged, and Nick would be there, waiting for him to make a mistake. He'd waited three years to get this close to the information he needed; he could wait a few days longer.

Behind the station where the baristas were taking orders and preparing fancy custom coffee drinks, it was buzzing like a beehive. Like a well-oiled machine, the employees shouted drink orders to each other: single shot this, no-foam that, half-caf the other. Even one of the employees could be his guy. They all got breaks during their shifts. Anyone of them could go in the back where they kept supplies and spend a few minutes on a computer. It would be a great cover. And who would suspect a minimum-wage barista?

"Double shot, no-whip mocha for Nick."

Upon hearing his drink called out, Nick pivoted and snatched his overpriced coffee from the bar.

"Ouch!" he hissed and set it back down.

"Sleeves." The employee behind the counter pointed to a basket with cardboard cup protectors, before calling out the next drink. "Triple shot, grande latte for Michelle."

"Thanks." He slipped a sleeve around the hot paper cup, took his drink, turned on his heel—and instantly froze.

Only his extremely fast reaction saved him from colliding with the young woman who'd approached the counter for her latte. Instead, Nick jerked backward, hitting the counter with his back. The impact made him involuntarily tighten his grip on his coffee cup. The plastic lid popped off and the hot mocha splashed over the rim, spilling over the front of his T-shirt.

"Shit!" he cursed as the hot liquid touched his skin.

Instinctively jerking back from the burning coffee, his elbow hit something behind him. Nick shot a look over his shoulder just as the latte the barista had called out for the next customer spilled onto the counter.

"Well, great!" the woman he'd nearly crashed into grumbled beneath her breath. "I really needed that latte."

Yeah, and he needed not to be making a spectacle of himself. *Way to stay under the radar, Nick.*

Setting his half-spilled drink onto the counter, he flashed the barista who was already cleaning up the mess a quick smile. "So sorry, I'll pay for it, of course."

"No worries, I'll make another one." She looked past him. "Michelle, just a minute, okay?"

"Thanks," the female customer—Michelle presumably—answered.

Nick nodded. "Much appreciate it. But I'll pay for it."

He turned around to face the woman the barista had addressed and froze once more, when he caught something flashing silver. Instinctively, he focused on the pendant around her neck. A spotlight from the ceiling reflected off the shiny surface, giving it emphasis when at any other time Nick wouldn't have given the item a second glance. It was probably not even made of silver, maybe just of steel or aluminum. But its shape was undeniable: it was a tiny Guy Fawkes mask, the same kind the hacker cooperative, Anonymous, used as their symbol.

This couldn't be a coincidence. What were the odds of somebody wearing this type of keepsake in the same coffee shop he'd traced the hacker to? Nick was no betting man, but he would put his money on this woman.

Slowly, he lifted his eyes and looked at her for the first time.

His breath hitched, air fleeing his lungs. Red lips was the first thing he saw. Full and plump, slightly parted, showing perfectly straight, white teeth. Her skin was olive as if she came from the Mediterranean. There was a golden sheen of perspiration on her face. Not surprising, since it was muggy as hell in the city, and even in the air-conditioned interior of the coffee shop, it was warm.

Blue eyes framed by dark lashes looked at him, assessing, questioning, curious. But he didn't let that deter him from scrutinizing her, because it wasn't the ex-CIA agent in him inspecting her, it was the man in him, the one whose blood was rushing to his groin with a speed he couldn't quite comprehend. All he knew was that this woman intrigued him on so many levels, the least of which was a professional one.

In dark blond waves, her hair fell to her shoulders, drawing attention to her spaghetti-strap top with the built-in bra that accentuated her firm breasts— which were the perfect size for her lean five-foot-seven frame. Her cleavage was of the same olive skin as her face, a skin that tanned easily. And perhaps without tan lines. Not that his mind should go in that direction. After all, he wasn't here to pick her up. Not for any romantic reasons anyway. Though, of course, to further his mission, he needed to get close to her. Just how close he didn't know yet.

For an instant, he wished that this woman wasn't the hacker he was after, but simply a regular customer of the quaint coffee shop. But the pendant and the computer bag that was slung bike-messenger-bag-like across her torso suggested otherwise.

"Uh... sorry... uh..." he stammered, both to convey the hapless man, but also because for a second he did feel just a little bit tongue-tied at so much physical perfection. "Uh, Michelle, is it?"

She tilted her head to the side, suspicious now. "How——?"

He jerked his thumb over his shoulder. "The barista called out your latte; the one I spilled. Sorry about that again."

Michelle seemed to relax. "No worries." She motioned to his torso. "At least you spilled your drink on yourself and not on me."

Nick flashed a warm grin, knowing that it was one of his special assets, one that made women feel comfortable with him. "Yeah, bit clumsy of me, wasn't it?" He reached for a napkin from the counter and patted the stain on his shirt, but there was no way of removing it. All he could do was pat it as dry as possible. "Well, guess that one's ruined."

Michelle chuckled. "Brown looks good on you."

Nick winked and used her light-hearted response to draw her in further. "Yeah, sure, have your fun. Laugh at the guy who's just made a fool of himself in front of a pretty woman."

The resulting blush on her cheeks looked good on her and confirmed that his charm was working. This would be the angle he could use to get to her and find out what she knew. With a bit of luck, he'd know in a few days—maximum a week—whether she could help him get what he needed.

# 4

He'd called her pretty, and that made her smile. After the day Michelle had had so far, the stranger's compliment felt like soothing lotion on a sunburn. Her meeting with her blackmailer—yes, *blackmailer*, because that's what he really was, no matter what government agency he was working for—had left her rattled. The pressure was on. Either she produced, or she would land in jail, and that was a place she didn't want to go to.

She'd much rather be in the company of a cute stranger, even if said stranger was a bit clumsy. At least the guy was no threat to her. The only danger she faced from the brown-haired hunk who was smiling at her, was being doused with coffee. And that was something she could easily survive.

Michelle watched as he dumped the soiled paper napkins in the trash bin and grabbed a new lid for his half-spilled coffee, securing it on the cup.

"I don't mean to be pushy or anything," he suddenly said, "but can I buy you a biscotti or a muffin to go with your latte?"

Michelle shook her head. "That's really not necessary. Besides, it's not like I need the extra calories." Keeping a trim figure was hard enough since she spent most of her days and nights in front of her computer. She needed no sugar to jeopardize her health and weight.

A charming smirk, accompanied by a long look up and down her person, was his answer. "I'm sure you'll burn them off in no time."

She opened her mouth, not really knowing how to reply to that, when the barista interrupted.

"Michelle, your drink is ready."

Michelle nodded to the stranger and reached past him. "Thanks, Elise."

"Let me pay for that," the hunk insisted once more, pulling his wallet from his pocket.

"Not necessary," the barista replied. "Spills happen all the time. Besides, Michelle's a regular."

"Well then," he said, "thanks, and sorry again." He took a step away from the counter to let her pass.

Michelle took her drink and brought it to her lips, taking a first sip.

"Uh, Michelle."

She lifted her eyes above the coffee cup and looked at him, curious what else he wanted. "Yes?"

"I'm Nick, by the way. I'm new to the neighborhood." He offered his hand.

Hesitantly, Michelle shook it. "Hi, Nick. I'm Michelle, but then you already know that."

A broad grin made his face look younger than he seemed at first sight. She allowed herself to look at him more thoroughly now. He had a stubble beard, the kind a man who didn't have time to shave for two or three days would sport. It made him look rugged. His hair was medium-brown, but not dull. There was a healthy sheen to it. His eyes were green-brown, his skin on the light side as if he spent lots of time indoors. He wore a short-sleeved light-blue polo shirt and black cargo pants. Despite their loose fit, it was evident that his legs were muscular, just like his arms, though he didn't look like a bodybuilder. He was lean.

"Listen, I get it if you don't want to be seen with me." Nick motioned to his shirt. "Stains and all, you know." He grinned disarmingly. "But considering you made me spill my drink, maybe you could make it up to me by keeping me company while I finish what's left of my mocha?"

"Now *I* made you spill your drink?" She had to laugh at that.

"Yep. The moment I saw you, I lost all control over my body."

Michelle rolled her eyes and walked toward her favorite spot, a large armchair in one corner. Was Nick coming on to her, or was he just being overly friendly? "The way I remember it is that you didn't even see me. That's why you spilled your coffee."

He winked. "Darn, you got me." Then he suddenly leaned in, lowering his voice. "Normally that line works, you know, but I guess you're too smart for that."

Michelle laughed. She had no defenses against his boy-next-door charm. It was disarming. And non-threatening, and that's what she needed right now. Some normalcy in her life.

She motioned to the second armchair, while she slunk down in her favorite spot and set her computer bag down. "Guess I'm not getting rid of you that easily."

Nick sat opposite her and lowered his backpack to his feet. "I'm kind of like caramel, sticky but sweet."

She chuckled. "So that pick-up line… Has it actually ever worked for you?"

He shrugged. "I'm still refining it. Rome wasn't built in a day either."

"So that's a *no* then."

"Wow, do you always jump to conclusions this fast?"

"Only when the evidence is pretty clear."

Both sides of his mouth tilted up. "What are you, Michelle, some kind of detective?" He leaned across the small table between them and set his drink down. "Should I be afraid of you?"

"Should you?" She ran her eyes over him once more. Maybe he should be afraid of her. After all, he looked rather innocent, and she was anything but.

By all accounts, she was a criminal, though she'd never really seen herself that way. She'd been a hacker since she'd first surfed the internet. Exposing things the government wanted to hide from its people had been her mission in life. Anonymous had been her family, anarchy her religion. But all that was gone now, because she had to serve the very enemy she'd fought against for so long: the US government. She couldn't even run to her old friends, the other hackers, because doing so would only endanger them, expose them. She had to get out of this by herself.

Which begged the question why she was wasting time flirting with Nick. Because, yes, she was actually flirting with him. She would be better off getting back to work and trying to deliver the person *Deep Throat* was looking for.

However, everybody deserved a break once in a while. And what was the harm in talking to a nice guy for a few minutes? It was relaxing, and maybe this was the way to recharge her batteries and get a second wind for today.

"So you're a local," Nick said, just as she opened her mouth, talking over him, "You're new to the neighborhood?"

Embarrassed she chuckled. "Go ahead."

"No, no, you first," he insisted.

"Did you move here recently?"

"Yes, this week. I'm from a small town in Indiana."

Just as she'd thought: an innocent in the big city. "What brings you here?"

"Work. I needed a change of scenery."

She nodded. "Yeah, I get that." She wanted a change of scenery, too. Preferably a sandy beach in a country that didn't extradite to the US.

"You work here in D.C.? At the university?" he asked.

"At the university?" Her eyebrows snapped together.

He motioned to her computer bag. "You look like you could be a lecturer or something."

She smiled. If only she had a harmless job like that. "I think you need to work on your detective skills a little more," she joked. "I could be a student."

Flashing his white teeth, he said, "But you're not. Not that you look old, but you look a lot more serious than any student I've ever met."

"I could be a graduate student or a resident."

"Yes, but they are generally too tired to stay awake." He pointed at the young female doctor napping in a chair across from them. "Or too focused on their thesis." Nick pointed to a young man typing away on his laptop so furiously that she was wondering if either he or his computer would start smoking soon.

"Point taken," Michelle admitted, enjoying the little game they were playing more than she should.

"You're gonna keep me guessing, aren't you?"

"You seem to have fun. Don't most men like a challenge?"

"Guess so. But I'm just a country bumpkin from Indiana. And you're a sophisticated woman from the Capital. I've got the feeling you'd just be playing with me." He winked.

The country bumpkin routine she didn't buy at all, though it was cute, she had to admit. "You're quite the charmer, aren't you? Is that why you moved to D.C.? To try out your country charm with city women?"

"Something like that." He reached for his mocha and took a sip.

"So what do you do then?"

"For a living you mean?"

"Yeah, for a living. Unless, of course, you're independently wealthy and are just mingling with the working masses for kicks."

"I wish." He grinned. "But I'm a working stiff."

"And you're not gonna tell me what you do, right?"

"You strike me as the kind of woman who'd rather find out for herself. Am I right?"

"Are you trying to make yourself more interesting than you are?"

He leaned over the table, lowering his voice. "Is it working?"

She met him halfway. "I'll tell you once it is."

"Well, I'd better leave then, before we become too familiar and all my mysteriousness is going out the window." He rose quickly and grabbed his backpack. "It was nice meeting you, Michelle. Maybe I'll see you again sometime."

"Yeah, maybe."

She watched him as he marched toward the entrance door, his gait determined. His butt muscles flexed with each step, and she wondered what other moves he had. Moves she didn't mind him using on her. Moves of a more intimate nature. She licked her lips at the thought. It had been a while since she'd been with a man. Maybe that's what she needed to unwind: a passionate fling. It didn't have to mean anything. In fact, it was better if it didn't. Her life was too much of a mess already anyway. She didn't need a relationship to add to it.

At the door, Nick stopped, but before he pushed it open, he looked over his shoulder, grinning straight at her.

Embarrassed that he'd caught her staring, she took a sip of her lukewarm latte, pretending she hadn't watched him. But they both knew she had and with undeniable desire. Because, despite the brief interaction, there'd been a spark.

And maybe that spark could ignite something.

A quick fire.

A flame that would burn brightly before it fizzled out again just as quickly.

# 5

Nick had waited for the right moment for several days. It was time.

He'd done his homework and had found out where Michelle lived, what her routine was, who she met, where she shopped, and what she ate. Most of the information he'd gathered simply by following and watching her without her noticing him. The rest he'd gleaned from internet searches. There wasn't much online about her, almost as if somebody had taken great pains to wipe out her digital footprint. Either she'd done it herself or somebody in a high enough place had done it for her.

In either case, Michelle was on the path to becoming a ghost. Here today, gone tomorrow. Instinctively Nick knew he didn't have much time to make a move. Today he'd go to the coffee shop and ask her out. He'd use all his charm to get her into bed, and then he'd look at that precious computer of hers, the one she never left home without, the one she never let out of her sight, not even when she used the restroom at the coffee shop, when he'd seen plenty of other customers leaving their laptops unattended while using the facilities.

Freshly showered and shaved, Nick waited at the next pedestrian crossing for the light to change. Beside him several people waited while a woman jogged in place, her eyes pinned to the lights across the street.

The premonition came out of nowhere like it always did, though he didn't always know immediately what he was looking at. This time he did. He recognized her immediately: Michelle. She was leaving the coffee shop, bumping into a customer on the way out. The man was cursing at her, but Michelle didn't even turn her head as if she didn't notice him. She appeared distracted, with a worried look on her face. Something was bothering her.

Nick felt himself reach out his hand, wanting to wipe the worry from her face, but in his vision Michelle kept walking, approaching the intersection where the light turned at that moment. She only briefly looked to her right, before stepping into the crosswalk. She didn't even see the taxi coming from the left. It hit her and flung her into the air. Behind the cab, her body slammed onto the hard asphalt like a rag doll. He knew immediately that she was dead. Knew it with a certainty that sent a chill to his bones and froze the blood in his veins.

"No!" he cried out and pushed the vision aside.

Tossing a quick look to either side of him, he dashed through the intersection, darting between the cars, drawing vile curses of the motorists onto himself. But he didn't care. He had no time to lose, or Michelle would die.

Why he had the visions and when, or how they appeared, Nick didn't know. It was his special gift—and the reason he lived in hiding. But today, he would use his gift to save a human life. If he wasn't too late already.

The light backpack he always carried slung over one shoulder, Nick ran through the busy early afternoon crowd that clogged up the sidewalks, pushing people out of his way if they didn't let him pass quickly enough. Curses and angry shouts followed him, but he barely took any notice. He was close, so close. Just another two blocks to the coffee shop.

He raced down the sidewalk, briefly stepping onto the street when a wheelchair user blocked his way. A car honked at him, but he kept running, darting between two vehicles to make a right turn into the street where the coffee shop was located at the end of the block.

A man he recognized from the premonition approached the door of the coffee shop. The door almost hit him in the face as it was opened. The woman exiting was Michelle.

Shit!

From the corner of his eye, Nick saw something flash yellow. He snapped his head to the side. The cab was passing him.

"Michelle!" he called out at the top of his lungs, waving at her.

She neither heard nor saw him and kept walking, approaching that fateful crosswalk.

Nick launched into an even faster sprint, pushing off the hot asphalt with all his strength. His heart raced as his lungs worked overtime.

*Gotta get to her! Run! Damn it, run!*

"Michelle!" he cried out again, but a car honking drowned out his voice.

*A few more yards, just a few more. You can do it!*

He darted past a woman with a small child, catching up with the taxi. Ahead of him, Michelle stood at the crosswalk, looking to her right, away from him and the approaching cab. Everything seemed to happen in slow motion now. The cab approaching the intersection… Michelle lifting her foot to take a step into the street…

"Michelle!" Nick barreled toward her.

Michelle ripped her head in his direction, eyes wide, mouth open, freezing in her current position, one foot on the street, one on the sidewalk. Nick lunged for her, turning her sideways in a split second, away from the traffic, inserting himself between her and the taxi, which had just reached them.

He pushed her away from him, toward the middle of the sidewalk. He tried to pivot with her, but the mirror of the cab caught in the strap of his backpack, ripping it from him and swiping his arm. The impact knocked him sideways. Nick was slammed against a metal newspaper rack, his left arm and side taking the brunt of it. But he didn't have time to worry about that now, nor about the screeching tires or the excited shouts around him.

Instead he searched for Michelle. When he finally found her, she was in the middle of the sidewalk, upright, but visibly shaken. He ran his eyes over her, but saw no obvious injuries.

Relieved, he slumped to the ground and rested his back against the newspaper rack. "Thank God," Nick murmured to himself, air rushing from his lungs now.

"Jesus Christ!" Michelle ran toward him, staggering a little and looking shaken. "Oh my God!"

"You all right, Michelle?" He looked up at her.

She breathed heavily as she crouched down to him. "That cab would have hit me!" Her lips trembled. "If you hadn't been there…" She closed her eyes for a moment, swallowing hard.

He reached for her hand, but winced at the pain in his arm and side. He breathed through it, willing the sensation to subside.

Michelle's eyes flew open and she shot a look at his arm. "You're hurt. Don't move. I'll call an ambulance."

Instantly, Nick shook his head. "I don't need an ambulance. I'm fine."

He didn't want an ambulance. Nor did he want a police report about the incident. While he had built a fake identity for himself, he wasn't about to test how well he'd covered his tracks.

Several bystanders crowded around. A man pushed through them: the taxi driver.

"You all right, buddy?" he asked, his voice shaking.

Nick quickly nodded.

"Shit!" The cabbie ran his hand over his head. "You stepped right in my path. Wasn't my fault."

A few pedestrians grunted angrily.

"Typical cab driver!" one of them cursed.

Nick used his good arm to push himself off the ground and, using the newspaper rack for leverage, pulled himself up. "I'm fine. Nothing happened." He pasted a thin smile on his face, nodding to the cab driver once more. "I'm all right. No need to hang around."

"You need a doctor to look at you. You could have a concussion," Michelle insisted.

Nick put his hand on her forearm and squeezed it. "I'm fine. Trust me."

The cab driver tossed him an unsure look, scratching his neck. "You sure? You not gonna sue me afterward?"

"I'm not gonna sue you. It was entirely my fault."

Finally, the cab driver marched back to his taxi. Nick turned to the other pedestrians who continued to hover, making sure they didn't miss anything.

"Honestly, nothing more to see here," he insisted and made a shooing motion.

"Is that your bag, ma'am?" A kid pointed to a computer bag on the sidewalk.

Michelle nodded and the boy handed it to her. "Thank you."

Slowly, the people disbursed. Nick glanced around. It was possible that somebody had already called 9-1-1 and the police were on their way. It was best not to risk hanging around here any longer. He reached for his backpack, glad to see that it was still intact from landing on the curb.

"Somebody has to look at you," Michelle said beside him.

He smiled at her, her concern touching him. "It's just a little bruise. I'll survive."

"Please, let's get you to a hospital."

"I can't. I don't have health insurance right now." It was true, although that wasn't the reason he didn't want to see a doctor. "I just need to ice down the area."

Michelle let out an annoyed huff. "Damn it, do you have to be so stubborn?"

He grinned. "You think I'm stubborn?"

She rolled her eyes. "Well, then let's go to my place. I'll look at your injuries and I swear if I think it looks bad, I *will* deliver you to the hospital myself."

At her bossy statement, Nick felt like saluting as if she were a drill sergeant in the army. But he suppressed the urge. "Yes, ma'am."

# 6

At least Nick wasn't objecting to her helping him.

"Can you walk?" Michelle asked, looking him up and down.

"I can. Where do you live?"

She motioned toward the path she'd originally been heading down. "It's not far. Just a few blocks."

Michelle hoisted her computer bag over one shoulder and waited for the light to change to green, letting out another breath. She was still shaking, but the reality of what had just happened was settling in. She'd been about to cross the street without looking. And had Nick not been there, she would have walked right into the path of the taxi. Everything could have been over in seconds. She shuddered at the thought.

"You okay?"

At Nick's concerned voice, she lifted her face to him. "I guess it's only just now sinking in. I can't believe I was so careless. It was so lucky that you were there. How did you realize—"

Nick took her hand in his and squeezed it. "Don't think about it any longer. It'll just drive you crazy. I'm happy that I caught you in time."

At the odd phrasing of his words, she snapped her eyebrows together. "Were you looking for me?"

"Actually, I was on my way to the coffee shop, hoping that I might see you, when I saw you at the intersection."

"Oh." It was odd since they hadn't seen each other since their first encounter a few days earlier.

"Yeah, when I saw you there, I realized you'd already left the coffee shop, so I called out to you." Nick grinned, shrugging. Then he motioned to the changed light, and together they crossed the street. "Took me a few days to scrape together all my courage to ask you out for coffee. I didn't wanna waste that opportunity. So I ran to try to catch up with you."

Her heart started beating faster, and this time it wasn't out of panic or shock. "You wanted to ask me out for coffee?" And instead he'd saved her from getting hurt.

Nick cast her a sideways glance. "Figured I'd try my country bumpkin charm on you once more; see if it works better this time."

In disbelief, she shook her head. Was this man for real? Not only was he a hero, saving her without regard for his own safety, but he was also self-deprecating, sweet, and absolutely charming. Not to mention handsome and sexy as hell. She quickly glanced at his hands. And apparently still single. Jesus, why could she not have met a guy like him earlier, when her life hadn't started to careen out of its tracks?

"I don't know what to say." She reached for his arm.

Wincing, he said, "No need to say anything. But a bag of ice would be great right about now."

"So sorry," she apologized when she realized that she'd just squeezed his injured arm. "Let's get you inside, and then I'll take care of your arm."

She pointed to a three-story brownstone. "I'm afraid it's a walk-up."

"Nothing wrong with my legs."

Michelle turned to the door and unlocked it. She entered, Nick on her heels, and walked ahead of him, climbing the old creaking staircase.

"You live alone?"

She looked over her shoulder. "Yes, it's just a small one-bedroom, cheap enough so I don't need a roommate."

"Good."

For an instant, her heart stopped. Was it wise to bring a man she'd only met for the second time today to her apartment? Was she inviting trouble by letting him into her place, where they would be alone? After all, she knew nothing about him.

Nothing apart from the fact that he was charming—which apparently serial killer Ted Bundy had been, too—and that he'd saved her life. That latter part helped her make up her mind. Nick had risked his own life to save hers and gotten injured as a result. She owed him to at least make sure he was all right. And she couldn't blame him for not wanting to go to a hospital. Without insurance, they would charge him an arm and a leg just for getting an x-ray and an icepack.

"Here we are," she announced as she reached the top floor and stepped onto the landing. There were two apartments on this floor. She pulled her key ring from her computer bag and inserted the key in the lock.

When she pushed the door open, she turned and saw Nick hesitating in the hallway. She waved him in. "Come in, I won't bite."

He smirked. "Promise?"

Michelle dropped her keys onto the side table in the short hallway from which one door led to the bathroom and the other to the bedroom. Ahead of her, an arch led into the living room with an adjacent tiny kitchen. It wasn't much, but at least she had privacy here.

"Nice place," Nick commented and followed her into the living room.

"Take a seat. And take off your shirt," she demanded and marched into the kitchen.

The door between living room and kitchen had long been removed because of lack of space. She opened the freezer and rummaged through it, finally finding a bag of frozen peas. It would have to do. She snatched a clean dish towel from a drawer and turned back to the living room only to slam to a halt.

Nick stood in the door frame, his chest bare and glistening. He was even better built than she'd suspected the day she'd first met him. In fact, he was positively ripped. Her mouth started watering at the sight of his six-pack-abs and the well-defined pectorals that seemed to twitch.

The only sound she managed to produce from her dry throat was *"Uh."* Great, she was turning into a drooling teenager. How pathetic.

"Sorry, didn't mean to startle you." The deep timbre of his voice bounced off the walls of the tiny kitchen.

In the small room he looked even more imposing, even more attractive, more tempting.

"Is that the ice?"

He motioned to the bag of peas, prompting her to spring back into action.

"Yes, yes. Sorry, I don't have real ice cubes, but this'll do the trick." She turned sideways. "Why don't you sit down here then, and I'll look at you." Not that she wasn't already *looking* at him. Or better yet, *ogling* him.

He squeezed past her to the single barstool next to the miniscule breakfast counter that was just big enough for one person. Awkwardly, she turned to try to avoid brushing against him, but it happened nevertheless.

A bolt of adrenaline shot through her at the unexpected contact. The accompanying heat wave scorched her from the inside, adding to the stifling temperature in her top-floor apartment. Right now, she wished for air conditioning, though she wasn't sure it would help cool her body down.

Nick took a seat on the barstool and turned toward her. She placed the bag of frozen peas on the counter and reached for his arm.

"I'm just gonna touch your arm lightly to see if it's broken, okay?"

He only nodded, but remained silent. Michelle felt his eyes on her and tried to remain calm. It was only natural that he was watching what she was doing, she told herself. In his situation, she would do the same. It didn't mean that he was checking her out. Besides, he was probably in pain, and not even men had romantic feelings when in pain, right?

Slowly, she ran her hands over his arm. His forearm felt fine, and when she squeezed hesitantly, he didn't protest. When she reached his elbow, she tested his range of motion, and again, nothing struck her as odd.

"All good," he commented.

She brushed her hand over his upper arm and applied a little bit of pressure. Instantly, Nick jerked back and groaned.

"Sorry." She caught his gaze. "I need to check a little more."

"Mmm-hmm." His eyes were unreadable. Had they turned darker?

The warmth of Nick's skin made her fingers tingle. She took a steadying breath, hoping he didn't notice how touching him affected her. Hell, she was no blushing virgin! He wasn't the first man she'd touched. He wouldn't be the last either. Though it had been a while since she'd been with somebody. Maybe too long. Perhaps that was the reason why touching him got her all flustered.

Pulling herself together, she continued examining his arm. Even though he hissed when she squeezed his bicep, she didn't think his arm was broken.

"I think it's just bruised. It'll probably turn blue in a day or two." She exchanged a look with him.

"Just as I thought. Thanks."

"Hold on," she said. "How about your ribs?" She pointed to his side. "You crashed against the newspaper rack quite hard. Lift your arm."

Nick followed her command and she placed her hand over his side, pressing lightly.

He shrank back. "Okay, that's enough playing doctor for one day," he said lightly, though his facial expression told her that he'd gotten bruised there, too.

Michelle tilted her head. "And there I was having so much fun," she said sarcastically. She sighed. "Honestly, men."

She grabbed the bag of peas and placed it over his upper arm. "Hold this."

While he pressed the makeshift icepack to his bicep, she wrapped the dish towel around it then knotted it. "That should do."

She opened the freezer again and snatched a bag of sweet corn from it. "This is for your ribs. You're gonna have to press it against your side for a while."

"Aye, aye, ma'am."

She braced her hands at her hips. "And don't make fun of me. I'm just trying to help you, you stubborn idiot." She sniffed in a short breath.

"So I'm an idiot now?" he asked way too softly—almost as if he knew what was going on inside her.

Tears sprang to her eyes. Nick could have gotten killed today. *For her.* For saving her miserable life, when she knew her life was practically forfeit anyway. Because if she couldn't produce the results Mr. Smith wanted, he'd have her thrown in prison. And right now, she was at a dead end. As if somebody had put a wall up right in front of her. One she couldn't penetrate. She was running out of options and out of time.

"Why did you do that?" A sob tore from her chest. "That cab could have killed you! You don't even know me. You don't even know whether I'm worth risking your life for. You idiot." The last word barely made it over her lips, tears choking off her voice.

She felt his hand wrap around her wrist a moment later, pulling her to him. His arm came around her back, dragging her closer until she was captured between his spread legs, chest-to-chest with him.

He used his forefinger to tip her face up so she had to look at him. "Every life is worth saving." He paused, smirking. "As for calling me an idiot: I'd like an apology for that." His gaze dropped to her mouth.

Her breath instantly hitched, awareness permeating every cell of her body. Her pulse began to race, and perspiration slicked her skin.

"A really nice, long apology." He dipped his head until his lips were floating just an inch above hers. "How about that apology now?"

His voice was drugging, his strong arm imprisoning her. His breath blew against her face, tempting her further.

"Just one kiss," she murmured.

"Two. You called me an idiot twice."

"Two then."

The moment the last word left her mouth, she felt Nick's lips on hers. At first the touch was soft and gentle, a mere brushing of skin on skin, of warmth sliding against warmth. Instinctively her lips parted as she took in his masculine scent, inhaling his aroma, taking it deep into her lungs. A pleasant shiver ran down her spine, making her tremble in his arms.

An appreciative hum came from his lips, reverberating against hers, the vibrations spreading a tingling sensation over her mouth and face.

She knew then that two kisses wouldn't be enough to satisfy the sudden hunger that was growing inside her.

# 7

Nick tilted his head and captured Michelle's lips fully, tasting her drying tears and her sweet breath. Her sudden emotional outburst had taken him by surprise, yet at the same time given him the chance to do what he knew he had to: get close to her so he could find out what she knew. He pushed the twinge of guilt that surfaced to the back of his mind. Deep down he knew this was wrong, but he couldn't stop himself.

Seeing her die in his vision had been too real, and knowing that had he arrived only two seconds later, the vision would have come true, still sent chills down his spine. That was a feeling he couldn't ignore. What he needed now—what they both needed—was a few moments of sheer and utter abandon. A brief celebration of life, of lust and passion, of tenderness and ecstasy. For a short while, he would forget what his real mission was and concentrate on only one thing: making the woman in his arms forget the fact that she'd narrowly escaped death today.

He wanted to shower her with passion, make her body hum with pleasure, and lose himself in her. Just for a short time. That part wouldn't be a lie. It would be real and honest.

Nick ignored the pain in his side and focused only on Michelle, on the softness of her lips, the delicious taste of her mouth, the insistent strokes of her tongue as she dueled with him in a match that neither could win. *Hunger* was the word that came to mind when her hands dug into his shoulders, holding on to him for dear life as if she was afraid he'd toss her to the side.

He slid his hands down below her waist, feeling her firm ass through the thin fabric of her summer skirt. Goddamn it, was she wearing anything underneath that thin scrap of cotton? It felt like she was naked.

Nick growled involuntarily, intensifying his kiss, while he pressed her against his groin, where his cock was already as hard as a crow bar.

Michelle moaned into his mouth, her body stiffening for an instant. Yes, she could feel his erection, knew what was coming, because a kiss wouldn't suffice now. He needed more from her. He needed to be inside her to make the horrors of the last hour vanish. To make him forget.

Impatiently, he slid his hands underneath the fabric of her skirt. He nearly jumped out of his pants when he felt bare skin beneath his fingers. He palmed her ass, exploring her, and realized she was wearing a thong. He should have known that a hot woman like Michelle wore sexy underwear like that. Not that at this moment he needed any additional turn-on in the form of sexy lingerie.

Michelle kissing him with such unrestrained passion was turn-on enough. And Michelle rubbing herself against his cock was almost too much. But she was doing it, and he wasn't going to stop her. Just as she wasn't stopping him when he pulled her thong down to her thighs until it finally dropped to her feet.

Now he had full access to her sex and made use of it. He slid his hand down her ass to the juncture of her thighs, reaching between them. She complied immediately and widened her stance so he could bring his hand between her legs.

She was warm and wet there. A drop of her juices coated his finger and he rubbed it along her moist cleft. She jolted under his intimate touch, but didn't pull back. Instead, she rocked her pelvis against his cock as if asking for more.

Nick ripped his lips from hers. "You want that, yeah? You want my cock?"

Passion-clouded eyes stared at him. Her face was flushed, and she dropped her lids, but he wouldn't allow her to evade him. "Look at me."

Her eyes flew open and she pinned him.

"Do you want that?" He rocked his cock against her and rubbed two fingers along her wet sex, gently probing at the entrance to her body. "Do you want me inside you?"

"Yes." She put her hand on his nape and pulled him back to her so there was only a sliver of space between them. "I want you. Now. Here."

Just as well that he was prepared for this. He'd shoved a couple of condoms into his pants pocket before leaving his place. Those would come in handy now.

"Good, 'cause that's what I've wanted to do from the moment you made me spill my mocha."

"I didn't make you spill your mocha."

"Did, too."

He captured her lips again, stopping her from voicing any further protest. Kissing her, Nick lifted her off her feet and spread her legs, wrapping them around his waist. He marched into the living room, his cock sliding against her center with every step. The thrilling sensation even made the pain in his arm fade into the background.

When he reached the sofa, he laid her onto it and lowered himself between her thighs. He didn't lose any time and lifted her skirt to expose her now naked sex. The sight robbed him of his breath. She was entirely bare. Nothing was hidden from his view.

"Baby," he groaned.

How was he going to survive this? Another few seconds and he'd come right in his pants. *Fuck!* He had to get himself under control.

Nick lifted his gaze and met Michelle's eyes. "You're absolutely gorgeous." Then he lowered his head, but continued to keep eye contact. "I hope you don't mind, but I skipped lunch. And I love buffets." And the kind of feast that was spread out in front of him was impossible to resist. "All you can eat, you know."

Her breath hitched before he lowered his mouth to her smooth folds and took his first taste. Slowly he licked over her bare skin and gathered up the dew that was trickling from her. With his hands on her thighs, he spread her wider.

"Open up for me," he coaxed and suckled along her delicious folds.

Michelle spread her legs wider, lifting one over the back of the sofa.

"There you go. Just like that." He scooped his hands under her ass and tilted her pelvis toward him. Then he dove back to her sex and sucked her like a man who hadn't eaten in days.

Michelle was so easy to read. Every moan and sigh, every move she made told him what she liked and what she craved more of. He adjusted to her wishes, licking her more gently now, with longer strokes. She was getting wetter with every second, her moans becoming louder and more frequent. Her hands tugged at her spaghetti top, and he realized that she was perspiring.

Nick lifted his head from her and helped her rid herself of her top and the skirt. When she finally lay naked before him, he swept his eyes over her. She was as sexy as sin itself. And the fact that he was still wearing his pants made the whole situation even more exciting.

Nick took her hand and pulled it to the front of his pants, pressing it against the erection that pulsed there. "Feel what you do to me."

Michelle pulling her lower lip between her teeth nearly made him spill, or was it the fact that she squeezed his cock right at that moment? It didn't matter. What mattered was getting rid of his clothes, or there would indeed be a disaster on the horizon.

He lifted himself off the couch and shucked his shoes, then unzipped and pulled his pants off. When he hooked his thumbs into the waistband of his boxer briefs, he met her eyes. She stared at him with open desire.

"Yes, look at my cock. Look at what you'll feel inside you in a moment." Slowly he pulled his boxer briefs down and revealed his erection.

When he saw the look of admiration and eager anticipation on her face, pride swelled inside him. He would make sure that look turned into one of satisfaction and ecstasy shortly.

Reaching for his pants, he pulled a condom from the pocket and ripped open the packaging.

"You came prepared."

At her words, he snapped his gaze to her. Michelle was propping herself up on her elbows, her nipples pointing at him.

"Can't blame a guy for hoping he'd get lucky."

She smiled softly. "Is that what you call it?"

He slowly rolled the condom over his hard-on. "What would you call it then?"

Michelle gave his cock a pointed look. "Maybe *I'm* the one who's getting lucky."

Nick threw his head back and laughed. "A woman after my own heart." Then he lowered one knee onto the sofa. "So, tell me, what would you like? I'm open to suggestions, because frankly, as long as I get to be inside you, I don't care which way."

"Stop talking." She dropped back into the cushions and crooked her finger, inviting him to come closer. "Just let me feel you."

"Yes, ma'am."

With a grin that was surely going to become permanent, Nick lowered himself between her legs, bringing his cock to her center. Guiding himself along her moist sex, he allowed her warm juices to coat the condom.

When she moaned and arched her back off the sofa, he slid his cock over her clit, teasing the tiny organ. If he had any self control left, he'd finish her off by licking her clit until she came, but that was something that would have to wait for another time, because right now he couldn't wait another second to be inside her.

"Tell me you want my cock," he demanded.

Her hand came up and wrapped around his nape, pulling him down to her. "I want to feel your cock inside me. And if you don't do it right now, I'm going to scream!"

"Michelle, let's get one thing straight: you're going to scream either way," Nick promised and plunged inside her, seating himself until his balls slapped against her flesh.

He watched with male satisfaction how her eyes closed and all the air rushed from her lungs, how she pulled her lower lip between her teeth and how her hand tightened around his nape, her fingernails clawing into him. Even the little bit of pain he welcomed.

When he withdrew to thrust again, he felt his injured side, felt the pain in his arm and ribs, noticed how the icepack was sliding down his arm and tossed it aside. There was time later to ice his wounds. Right now, he needed to make love to the gorgeous woman beneath him. That was his only focus.

Shifting most of his weight to his uninjured side, and bracing himself on his knees and one elbow, he began to move inside her. God, she felt good. Smooth, warm, welcoming. She enveloped him like a glove, like a tight bandage that caressed and soothed at the same time. Her interior muscles were tight and strong, holding him like a vise.

Nick brushed a strand of her dark blond hair from her face and gazed into her eyes. "So beautiful." And yet she was his enemy, though she didn't know it, had no inkling of who he was or why he was here. In a way, it made her an innocent. He was the predator. A predator who wanted nothing more than to please the beautiful creature in his arms. Who wanted nothing more than to make her feel pleasure and satisfaction. Who wanted nothing more than to feel her submit and give herself to him if only for a few moments.

He threw his head back. Goddamn it, he didn't want her to be the enemy. He didn't want to have to use her. And, at that moment, he wished for nothing more than to be wrong about his suspicion that Michelle was the person who'd been chasing him online. But all evidence pointed to her. The Guy Fawkes pendant that even now dangled around her neck mocked him, even though its bearer knew nothing of the turmoil she was causing him.

"Oh God, Michelle!" he cried out and took her harder. Almost as if to punish her, when in reality he wanted to punish himself.

"Nick! Oh yes!" She rocked against him, her tempo increasing, her breathing erratic.

He tore his eyes from the pendant, trying not to think about it, and looked at Michelle's glowing face instead. Beads of sweat formed on her forehead, giving her skin an enticing sheen. Her lips were parted, tempting him to capture them for another kiss.

"I haven't had my second kiss yet," he murmured.

A soft laugh burst from her lips then. "But you did." She lowered her gaze, and he immediately realized what she was referring to.

"Oh that." He winked. "That was just a quick taste. Maybe later I'll get a longer one?"

Her hand came up, and she stroked her index finger over his lower lip. "Are you for real?"

"As real as it gets."

Before his conscience could intervene, he took her lips for a hard kiss, trying to prove to himself that he was making love to Michelle because he was attracted to her, not because he needed to find out what she knew. And why shouldn't he be attracted to her? She was beautiful, sexy, and full of life. And she felt good in his arms. It had been a while since he'd felt like this, since he'd felt he could let himself go and indulge in this very physical pleasure without having to look over his shoulder to see who was after him.

The way Michelle responded to him made everything male in him come to life. In her arms he was only a man, not the ex-CIA agent who could see future events, not the man who would kill to protect his life and that of his fellow agents, the ones who'd gone underground to survive. No, in Michelle's arms, he was only a man who wanted to feel the love of a woman, even if it was only physical and fleeting. But he needed this, needed to feel the connection of his body to hers. To feel alive again and not like the ghost he'd become.

Michelle was giving him this, was showing him what life could be like again if only he defeated his enemies. With her tantalizing body, Michelle gave him what he craved most: a place where he was safe and welcome.

Harder and harder he took her, his quest for release more urgent now. He shifted his angle, watching for signs from Michelle to make sure she would climax with him.

Severing the kiss, he lifted his head and gazed into her eyes. Heavy-lidded she looked back at him.

"Baby, you feel so good. So amazing." He clenched his jaw, realizing how imminent his orgasm was. "I'm close. Tell me what you need."

She bucked toward him. "Harder."

He complied with her wish, pulling back his hips and slamming into her. His neck muscles strained as he tried to hold on to his control while repeating the action again and again.

"Yes!" she cried out and arched off the cushions, offering her breasts to him.

He took the offering and dipped his face and sucked one hard nipple into his mouth, closing his lips around it. Beneath him, Michelle trembled, and her interior muscles clamped down on him, imprisoning his cock in her warm channel.

A shudder raced through his entire body, and a bolt of energy shot into his balls, sending hot semen through his cock. He exploded, joining her in her climax, rocking with her as they both came down from their high. Floating blissfully, without thought, without worries…

Breathing hard, he sank down onto her, his knees shaking from the intensity of his orgasm, his heart racing like a bullet train, his side and arm aching now.

Michelle blew out a breath. "Wow."

"Yeah, wow," Nick replied.

# 8

Nick pressed a kiss into Michelle's hair. He'd pulled her on top of him on the couch, not wanting to crush her with his weight. He liked the feel of her warm body as she lay there, relaxed and breathing evenly.

"Are you falling asleep?" he asked, chuckling.

"Mmm."

"Guess I must have bored you."

She lifted her head and smiled at him. "You've worn me out, that's what you did, and you know it." She pressed her cheek back onto his chest.

He liked how easy she was to talk to. If he weren't on the run, he wouldn't mind having a girlfriend like Michelle, maybe even a serious relationship.

"I think you've got it the wrong way 'round. *You* wore *me* out."

She laughed softly, and her breath ghosted over his nipple, to his own surprise hardening it in an instant. Fuck, he still wanted more. Taking her just once hadn't been quite enough.

"Are you complaining?" she asked.

He gave her a good-natured slap on her ass. "No complaints. Just an observation."

She wiggled on top of him, and he palmed her ass with both hands, stopping her from rubbing herself against his cock.

"Go ahead, keep doing that, and I'm gonna have to bend you over that armchair and teach you some manners," he warned and pressed another kiss on the top of her head.

She lifted her head and laughed. "Who says I have no manners? Didn't I take care of your injuries like a good little nurse?"

Nick lifted one side of his mouth into a smirk. "More like a naughty little vixen luring me into her lair so she can devour me. Remember, I'm just an innocent boy from Indiana. I have no defenses against experienced women from the city."

"Not even you believe that. You don't strike me as innocent. And I wasn't the one doing the seducing. I remember distinctly that you were the one asking for a kiss."

"True, but I had no idea you'd rub your hot little body all over me, making me lose all control. And there I'd planned on taking you out for a coffee, trying to get to know you better." He looked at his watch. "Guess it's too late for that now. It's more like dinner time."

"So you really wanted to ask me out on a date?"

"Sure did." He lifted his hand, making an all encompassing sweeping motion. "Guess I've got it backwards. Normally, sex comes after dinner." He combed a hand through her hair, enjoying the silky feel of it. "Though, if you don't object, I'd like to take you out for dinner now."

Her eyes widened. "You mean, even though you've already gotten what you wanted?"

"Who says I have?" He winked.

"Normally, guys make themselves scarce once they've gotten a girl into bed."

"Way I see it, we're not in bed." He patted the sofa cushion. "I believe this is a couch. And who says all I want is sex? I think you'd be selling yourself short if you thought that."

He looked deep into her blue eyes and felt how his heart started beating out of control. He wasn't lying to her. She did have a lot to offer—to the right guy. Unfortunately, he wasn't that guy, although if circumstances were different, he wondered if he could be.

"You really know how to turn on the charm," Michelle said.

"I do my best." Then he gave her another slap on her backside. "Now, how about that dinner date, or were you just gonna use me for sex and then toss me out on my ass?"

For far too long she looked at him, contemplating her answer. He shifted, his pulse kicking up. What was going through that pretty little mind right now? Best to grab the bull by the horns and turn things around.

"Oh my God, you actually have to think about that!? Way to boost a guy's self-confidence." He pulled himself up to sit, laughing, when Michelle started snickering.

"Sorry, couldn't help myself. I love it when a guy gets all flustered and insecure."

Nick planted a kiss on her nose. "You're a strange woman, Michelle."

She opened her mouth for a protest, but he put his finger over her lips, stopping her.

"Just as well that I have very peculiar tastes."

When her eyes softened and her lips curved up, he knew he'd won.

"Do I have time for a shower before dinner?" she asked.

"Take all the time you need."

She lifted herself up and stood. He couldn't help running his eyes over her body, admiring her firm breasts, her slim waist and soft hips, her long legs, and everything in between. When she turned to give him a view of her shapely ass, he groaned, wishing he could shower with her, but he had something more important to do.

"Do you mind if I switch on the TV while you shower?" he asked.

Michelle looked over her shoulder and pointed to the coffee table. "If you can figure out the remote, help yourself."

Nick reached for the black device and gave her a mock-chiding look. "I'm a guy. We invented remotes."

Shaking her head, Michelle disappeared down the hallway. Moments later, he heard the water running in the shower.

Nick jumped up, pressed the TV power button and turned up the volume, not even looking what channel was on. He gathered his clothes and dressed in fifteen seconds. Now he was ready.

He quickly scanned the living room, knowing instinctively he'd find nothing of importance here. Nevertheless he did a cursory search of the few drawers and surfaces anyway. It turned up nothing. His next stop was Michelle's bedroom. The door was opposite the bathroom door, which thankfully Michelle had shut. Nick now eased the door to the bedroom open and entered.

There wasn't much: a queen-sized bed, a dresser, night tables, a few boxes along one wall. The built-in closet was small and jam-packed with clothes, no files, no electronic equipment. Continuously listening to the sounds from the bathroom, Nick continued his search, opening the drawer of one nightstand. It was full of underwear. He rummaged through it, but only lingerie turned up.

He rounded the bed and searched the other nightstand. Several loose condom packages greeted him, together with tissues and lubricant. Nick grinned involuntarily. Good to know that Michelle had some extra supplies, just in case they burned through the few condoms he'd brought.

A quick perusal of the boxes turned up nothing but books and old photos. He checked his watch: Michelle had entered the bathroom three minutes earlier. He should have plenty of time to go through the rest of the apartment. He left the bedroom and stepped into the hallway. There, below the side table, lay her computer bag. He crouched down and opened it, tossing a quick glance to the bathroom door, listening intently. The water was still running.

The bag held a laptop, several cables, as well as notepads, pens, and the product tag for the bag itself. He pulled the laptop from its compartment and opened it. Though he was almost certain that Michelle wouldn't leave her computer unprotected, he had to find out if she'd, by some lucky chance, not password-protected it.

He booted up the machine, drumming his fingers on his thigh while he waited impatiently for the wheel to stop spinning. When the screen filled with color and presented him with the request to enter a password, he wasn't surprised. It would have been too easy. He quickly initiated the shut down and set the computer aside, looking through the bag once more. There had to be something.

He flipped through the notepad, but apart from some scribbles that looked like a shopping list, he didn't find anything. The moment the computer powered down, he slid it back into the bag. It didn't want to go in all the way, so he pulled it out again and checked. He found a piece of paper on the bottom of the compartment and looked at it. It was a manufacturer's warranty for a flash drive.

But where was it?

Shoving the computer back into the bag and closing it, Nick stood up. His eyes fell on the side table, where Michelle had tossed her keys when they'd entered her apartment. He picked the key ring up. Not only did it hold several keys, but a USB flash drive dangled from it.

"Gotcha," he murmured.

The sudden echo of his voice startled him. That's when he realized that the water wasn't running anymore. Michelle was done with her shower. He'd never met a woman who was that quick.

*Shit!*

# 9

Michelle wrapped the large bath towel around her still damp body and tucked in one end to hold it in place. Her hair was still wet, but she'd combed it. Considering the heat in D.C., it would dry in no time. With a last glance in the mirror, she turned the doorknob and opened the door.

She found Nick sitting on the couch—fully dressed now—staring into the TV. He turned his head.

"Hey," he greeted her with an easy smile.

"I'll be just a minute more," she told him. Her gaze fell on the TV and she had to do a double-take. "You're watching the Hallmark Channel?" What guy did that? Was Nick a true romantic at heart with whom she could actually watch sappy romances on TV? This was too good to be true.

Nick hastily reached for the remote. "Uh, no, ah, actually, I was just channel-surfing, trying to find ESPN." He pressed a button, and the channel changed. Then he moved to the next one in the lineup as if to prove that he told the truth.

Michelle chuckled. "Sure you were." She turned toward the bedroom.

"I was!" he called after her. "I was looking for a sportscast."

She didn't reply and walked into her bedroom, closing the door behind her. As she dropped her towel onto the bed and rummaged through her closet to find something appropriate to wear, she smiled to herself. Nick was unusual, she had to give him that. When they'd made love, he'd been intense and demanding, while simultaneously proving to be a very considerate lover, one who not only took care of her needs, but seemed to actually have a need to satisfy her. And he had. Satisfied her. Immensely.

But outside of bed, Nick was different: gentler, sweeter, almost shy. And he seemed embarrassed, almost flushed, when she'd caught him watching a made-for-TV romance, as if he didn't want to reveal that softer side of himself. A side she really liked.

Michelle slipped into a thin summer dress and took a matching cardigan from the hanger. She opted for high heels, wanting to feel sexy tonight. She inspected herself in the full-length mirror inside the closet door and twirled in front of it. She definitely looked presentable.

Taking a deep breath, she left the bedroom and walked back into the living room. The TV was off, and Nick wasn't sitting on the couch anymore. She turned on her own axis. Had he left without her?

"Nick?"

Footsteps coming from the kitchen made her turn. He came walking back into the living room, jerking his thumb over his shoulder.

"Hope you don't mind. I helped myself to some water."

Relieved, she exhaled. "Of course not. I'm sorry, I should have offered you something to drink earlier. I'm such a bad hostess."

He walked up to her, his eyes fairly drinking her in. "Oh, I wouldn't say that. You were very welcoming." He graced her with a smoldering look, one that made her knees tremble.

She wiped her suddenly damp hands on her dress, fidgeting.

"You look very nice," Nick murmured, taking another step closer that brought them chest-to-chest. With his index finger, he tipped her face up. "Absolutely stunning, in fact." He brushed his lips over hers in a feather-light kiss. "Now you're making me really hungry."

She swallowed hard, knowing he wasn't talking about food. And suddenly she didn't care about dinner anymore.

Nick took her by surprise when he stepped back and reached for her hand. "Let's go and have that first date, shall we?"

Almost disappointed that he hadn't thrown her down on the nearest flat surface, she followed him to the door. He took the small backpack that he'd tossed there upon entering her place and opened the door. Turning to the side table, Michelle grabbed her keys and shoved them into her handbag, then slung it diagonally across her torso, following Nick out and letting the door slide shut behind her.

Muggy air greeted her when she stepped outside and walked along the sidewalk next to Nick. Though it was still light, and would remain so for another few hours, dark clouds hung in the sky and she could almost smell the coming thunderstorm.

"Where are you taking me?" she asked, giving him a sideways glance.

Nick pointed in the distance. "It's only three blocks. Are you okay walking in those shoes or would you rather take a cab?"

She was touched by his concern. "I can walk, no worries."

"Good." He paused. "Tell me a little about yourself, Michelle. I'm curious about your life. Are you from D.C.?"

Hesitant to reveal anything about herself, she asked, "Are we doing twenty questions?"

"No, but we *are* on our first date, and from what I recall about first dates, people tell each other stuff like where they're from, what their favorite color is, things like that."

"From what you recall?"

"It's been a while since I've been on a date," he admitted, sounding almost embarrassed about it.

"How long?"

"Too long I guess, since it appears that the rules have changed since I last had one."

"The rules haven't changed," she admitted. "I just don't go on many dates."

"Well, we're a pair, aren't we?" He squeezed her hand and pulled it to his mouth, pressing a quick kiss on her knuckles. "So how about I start with something to break the ice?"

"I think we already broke the ice earlier."

Nick let out a belly laugh. "You're something, Michelle. I'm surprised no guy has snatched you up yet. Girls like you don't stay unattached for long."

She shrugged. "I'm not really the kind of girl who's looking for something permanent." It was a lie, of course, one she'd had to tell herself for a while now. Her life was way too chaotic to be thinking of settling down anytime soon.

"Mmm." Nick looked at her from the side.

To bridge the awkward pause that was building between them, Michelle asked casually, "So, what were you gonna tell me about yourself to break the ice?"

"What I do for a living. But if you're not interested, we can talk about something else."

"No, no, please. Tell me what you do."

"It'll probably sound boring. Maybe I should just make something up instead."

She stopped walking and turned to face him. "No, please don't. It can't possibly be all that boring. Besides, you don't have to impress me. You already got me into bed, remember?"

"How could I forget?" He winked and took her hand again to continue walking. "I work with computers."

"Doing what?"

"I make websites for people. You know, small businesses mostly. It's not a bad job, and I'm pretty good at it."

"That's great. You work for yourself, then?"

He nodded. "Independent contractor. I prefer that to being shackled to some company and having to be accountable to a boss."

"Yeah." Like she had to be accountable to Mr. Smith. And she hated that, hated that he was blackmailing her.

"How about you? What do you do?"

"Consulting," she shot back. "But I'm looking to make a change."

Like flee the country and disappear just as soon as she could set everything up and make sure Mr. Smith couldn't track her down. Until then, she had to play by his rules and execute his orders.

# 10

Nick felt the flash drive burn a hole in his pants pocket during the entire dinner at the cozy Italian neighborhood restaurant he'd taken Michelle to. Somehow he had to find a way to look at the contents of the flash drive, copy them, and put the memory stick back onto Michelle's key ring before she noticed it missing. Which meant that he had to continue being his charming self so Michelle would invite him back to her place after dinner.

It wasn't a hardship at all. Michelle was fun to be around. She had a quick wit and a sharp tongue, a wicked sense of humor, and an infectious laugh. Yet with every laugh they shared, with every eye contact they made, his guilty conscience grew. However, he had no choice but to continue his deception. Michelle could be the key to the information he needed, information that might save not only him and his fellow Stargate agents, but maybe thousands—if not millions—of people. He couldn't let his own feelings get in the way of the greater good.

If Michelle was the person who was trying to prevent him from accessing the CIA's secret servers, then she knew something and would be able to lead him to the person who'd destroyed the Stargate program and killed Henry Sheppard.

"Dessert?" Nick now asked, looking across the table at Michelle.

She shook her dark blond locks. "I'm too full."

"You sure?"

"Absolutely. How about we get out of here?"

He leaned over the table, lowering his voice to a seductive murmur. "I don't want the evening to end yet."

Her eyelashes fluttered. "It doesn't have to."

Her words sent a thrill through his core, and he snapped his head to the side, catching the waiter's eye. "Check, please."

When the waiter placed the tab in front of him, Nick pulled several bills from his wallet and placed them on the little tray.

"Do you always pay cash?" Michelle asked.

"My credit card got stolen last week. I'm waiting for the bank to send me a replacement," he lied.

In reality, he didn't use credit cards when he could avoid it. Cash was much harder to trace and safer if one wanted to stay off the grid.

"Ready?" he prompted Michelle and stood, offering her his hand to help her up.

"Ready."

As they walked to the exit, Nick eyed the signs to the restrooms. Now was the time, or things could get dicey for him later. He stopped.

"Sorry, do you mind if I stop at the restroom?"

"No, go ahead. Actually, I'll go, too."

Nick headed for the men's room and dove into the first stall. He sat down on the toilet, pulled his laptop from the bag and booted it up, while he pulled the flash drive from his pocket. The moment his computer started up, he unlocked it with his password, shoved the memory stick into the port, and copied the entire contents onto his hard drive. He had no time to look at what he'd copied, didn't even bother to shut down the computer properly or eject the stick safely, just slapped the lid shut and pulled the flash drive from the port.

A few seconds later, he left the stall and walked out of the restroom.

Michelle was already waiting for him. She smiled. "Beat you to it."

Nick shook his head in disbelief. "You can give a guy complexes, you know that?" He put his arm around her waist and guided her to the door of the restaurant.

The hostess opened it for them. "Thank you for your visit."

"Good night," Nick responded and walked out the moment a lightning bolt split the sky. Only a second later, thunder sounded above him, and the clouds opened up, unloading raindrops as thick as peas.

"Damn!" Michelle cursed, stopping under the awning in front of the restaurant.

Nick looked at her thin summer dress, which would most likely become transparent once soaked. And while he wouldn't mind that particular kind of view, he was sure she wouldn't appreciate it.

"I think we'd better try to get a cab."

"You've obviously never tried to get a cab during a D.C. downpour." She shook her head. "We'll be standing here all night. I say we make a run for it."

He looked at her with a newfound appreciation for her no-frills attitude. "You sure?"

"You chicken?"

"No, just a gentleman." He grinned and took her hand. "But since you clearly don't care about gentlemanly manners, I'll submit to your wishes."

Michelle winked at him. "Submit, huh?"

He rolled his eyes. "Don't get any ideas!"

He tugged at her hand, and they dashed out from underneath the protective canopy, running along the sidewalk.

Instantly they were doused from above as if they'd stepped into a shower stall, while passing cars splashed them from the side. There was no escaping the water.

Luckily, Nick knew that his computer was well protected in its water- and shockproof cover inside his backpack.

It didn't take them more than four minutes to bridge the distance from the restaurant to Michelle's apartment. When Michelle opened her handbag to dig for her keys upon reaching the main entrance of her apartment building, Nick stretched out his hand and took them from her.

"Allow me, milady!" he said gallantly and bowed in an effort to distract her.

"Playing knight now, are you?"

He turned toward the door, hiding what he needed to do by showing Michelle his back. "Knight in shining armor actually," he said jokingly, buying himself more time to hook the flash drive back onto the key ring. He turned the key in the lock an instant later and opened the door.

Michelle rushed inside and he followed, shaking off the excess water from his hair and body while the door fell shut behind him. Michelle was already climbing the stairs, eager to get to her apartment, and he hurried after her. Her wet dress showed every curve of her body, clinging to her like a second skin. Through it, he could see that all she wore beneath was a thong, no bra. The sight made him hard in an instant.

Arrived at the door to her apartment, Nick pulled Michelle into his arms, unable to hold back his desire for her a moment longer.

"Do you know how sexy you look just now?"

"I look like a drowned rat," she claimed, laughing.

"A very sexy drowned rat," he conceded and pressed her against the door, sinking his lips onto her hot mouth. Her lips parted immediately, allowing him to kiss her without restraint. Lust boiled up in him. Collecting all his remaining self control, he severed the kiss, breathing hard.

"We'd better get inside before we give your neighbors a show they'll never forget." He reached past her and inserted the key into the lock.

"You're a bad influence," Michelle said, but the sparkle in her eyes confirmed that she didn't consider this to be a bad thing.

Nick pushed the door open and nudged her inside. He tossed the keys onto the side table and kicked the door shut, before setting his backpack down. Then he pressed her against the wall beside the bathroom door.

"Yeah, a really bad influence," he mumbled and crushed her lips with his.

# 11

Her clothes were clinging to her, and Michelle knew she looked terrible, but it didn't matter, because Nick made her feel beautiful. His mouth was hungry on hers, his hands eager to free her of her wet clothes, his pelvis rocking against her with an urgency and rhythm that left nothing to her imagination.

With trembling hands she tugged on his shirt, pushed it up, so she could slide her hands along his naked skin and caress him. He shuddered under her touch, sending a thrill through her at the knowledge that she could bring this man to his knees.

For a brief instant, Nick released her lips and pulled his shirt over his head, revealing his muscled torso. Lust surged inside her, making liquid heat pool at her sex. Nick's hands were on her dress then, unzipping it in the back and pushing the fabric down to her waist. Another shove and the dress slid past her hips and pooled around her feet.

Her nipples were hard peaks, exposed to his view now because she didn't wear a bra. His eyes turned molten when he stared at her, his hands already reaching for her breasts, touching them, his knuckles sliding over her damp skin, making her shiver all over.

"Fuck, baby!"

Then his mouth was back on hers, his hands kneading her breasts, teasing her nipples, while farther below, he rubbed his erection against her center. But there was still too much fabric between them. She wanted all those barriers gone. She needed a skin-on-skin contact, needed to feel him as close as was humanly possible.

She pushed against him, made him step back a little so she could reach the button of his pants. She flipped it open then went for the zipper.

"Damn it, Michelle," he cursed when she pushed his pants and boxer briefs down to his thighs and freed his eager shaft. "I'm not gonna last."

"I don't care."

She pushed his pants down to his ankles and followed in the same direction, until her head was level with his cock. God, he was beautiful. Pumped full with blood, thick veins snaking up its sides, his hard-on demanded all her attention. Eagerly, she wrapped her hand around the root, gripping him firmly so he couldn't escape.

Nick groaned. She looked up and saw him bracing himself against the wall behind her with both hands, his eyes pinning her.

"If you're gonna do that," he said hoarsely, "then do it quickly while I still have an ounce of control left."

By the looks of his straining neck muscles, it wouldn't be long until he lost that self control. Already now Nick seemed like putty in her hands—rock-hard putty. And she rather liked that feeling. In fact, loved the power it gave her. The power to make a man surrender.

"Mmm." Michelle licked her tongue over the purple head of his glorious shaft and gathered up the moisture that had collected there. The salty taste spread in her mouth, making her hungry for more.

Nick let out a shuddering breath, while his hips jerked toward her. "I need... I need to..."

She knew what he needed and gave it to him. Her lips wrapped around the tip of his erection. Slowly, with her tongue along the underside of his cock, she descended on him, taking him as deep into her mouth as she could.

A loud moan bounced off the walls of her small hallway.

Gently, Michelle let his cock withdraw from her, before sliding down on him again. Her hand remained at his root, guiding him in and out. With every descent and every withdrawal she increased the speed and pressure. Nick's hips flexed in the opposite direction to hers, his cock thrusting into her mouth as she sucked him deeper.

"Fuck! Michelle!" he cried out, throwing his head back. "You've gotta stop."

But despite his impassioned plea, Nick continued moving his hips back and forth, fucking her mouth frantically. Eagerly, she licked and sucked him, moved her hand up and down the long stalk, ready to take what he was willing to give her, when he suddenly pulled back.

Her gaze shot up to him and she saw him breathe heavily. "I need a condom. Now!" He reached for her, pulled her up. "Do you have any?"

She motioned to the bathroom door. Before he could move—impeded by the pants around his ankles—she was already in the bathroom, rummaging through a drawer. When she turned around, condom in hand, he was behind her, fully naked now, stalking toward her.

He took the condom from her hand, ripped the package open with his teeth and rolled the latex over his cock, closing his eyes briefly and clenching his jaw as he did so. Then he pinned her with his eyes.

"Turn around," he ordered gruffly, motioning to the sink.

Without protesting, she pivoted. His hands were on her an instant later, bending her over the bathroom countertop.

Michelle lifted her head and watched in the mirror, how his passion-clouded eyes roamed over her backside. With a harsh exhale, he hooked his thumbs into the waistband of her thong and pulled it down to her thighs.

Then their eyes met in the mirror.

She felt the tip of his cock at her wet entrance, nudging her nether lips apart. His jaw tightened a moment before he plunged into her, seating himself balls-deep.

Michelle shuddered under the impact, but Nick's hands on her hips were holding her so tightly that she wouldn't slam into the counter despite his forceful move.

"See what you do to me?" he murmured and withdrew, only to thrust back into her with even more force.

"I thought you liked it," she teased, loving the knowledge that she was driving him wild. She liked this side of him, just as much as she liked his quiet, boy-next-door side.

"I love it," he confessed, meeting her eyes in the mirror. "Too much, in fact. Now you're gonna pay the price, baby."

It was a price she had no trouble paying. She loved the way he took her, like a man who knew what he wanted and didn't take no for an answer. Like a man who was used to his orders being followed. His gruff command to turn around hadn't turned her off in the least. On the contrary, it aroused her. To be dominated like this turned her on, made her wild, and awakened something primal in her, something entirely female.

"Yes, take me!" she cried out, not caring if that made her sound desperate or submissive. All she wanted was to be taken by him, to feel him pound into her with his cock until neither of them could move any longer.

"Yeah, I'll take you," he promised, bringing one hand around her hip to slide it to her front.

A wet finger on her clit made her gasp with pleasure. His hot breath at her ear, whispering to her made her close her eyes in anticipation.

"I'll fuck you until you come, and then I'll do it again, and again, and again. Is that what you want, Michelle, me taking you like this?"

"Yes," she choked out on a shallow breath. "Oh God, yes!"

She lost her ability to form a coherent thought after that. All she felt was Nick's cock sliding into her from behind, while his fingers strummed her clit as if it were a string instrument he wanted to tease a sound from.

When that sound finally came, it was a relieved outcry bursting from her lips, while her body shuddered under the power of her orgasm. Just before she collapsed, she felt Nick's cock spasm inside her, a loud moan accompanying his climax.

~ ~ ~

It always started with somebody handing him a tall glass of iced tea. It was no different this time. The hand, wrapped around the inviting beverage, came into view, though the person it belonged to never did.

Nick tried to force his head to turn this time, but his body didn't obey him. He only saw the cool liquid he so desperately needed and reached for it.

*Don't drink it!* he tried to scream to himself. But no sound came over his lips.

Instead, he lifted the glass to his lips and gulped down the ice-cold tea until only ice cubes were left. For a moment he closed his eyes, enjoying the cooling effect the drink had, but it was only temporary.

He knew where he was, and yet he didn't. The terrace of a large house. A garden beyond. Then the shore. Waves splashing against the narrow strip of sandy beach. An ocean maybe? Or a lake? A large one.

He gazed out onto it, following the ripples on its surface.

Only five sailboats were on the water despite the sunshine and the ample wind that filled their sails and propelled them forward. Why only five when the entire lake should be brimming with activity? When the houses to the left and right all had boat docks, and yachts waiting to be taken out onto the water. To be played with.

Did they know like Nick knew? Did they too sense the impending doom? Had they fled already, knowing it was too late to change the outcome?

"Please don't do this," Nick begged.

From behind him, a voice replied, "It's done."

But he couldn't accept that. He had to do what needed to be done.

His laptop sat on the wooden table, several windows open. Green computer code scrolled in one black window so fast, it looked as if it were raining numbers and letters.

His eyes blurred, and he tried to focus them, tried to make sense of it all. But his gaze drifted to the other window, the one that showed a video feed of a large concrete building. The angle was so narrow that he couldn't make out where the building was located. It could have been in the middle of a city or right in a desert, and Nick wouldn't have known.

In a third window, a clock was counting backward.

*Abort.* His lips formed the word automatically. He had to stop it. Save what was there to be saved.

From the corner of his eye, he noticed the white sails whizz by him. He spun his head in their direction and saw them fight against the increasing wind. But he knew if he didn't stop the countdown, they would have to fight against something even stronger than the wind. And they would lose.

"Abort," he whispered and lifted his hands to the keyboard, noticing all of a sudden how heavy they were, as if filled with lead. Like bricks, they landed on the keys, creating a row of gibberish among the scrolling code.

He willed his pinky to press the *escape* button to clear his typing, but his finger didn't move, didn't execute his brain's order.

*Do it, damn it!* Nick wanted to scream, but his tongue felt thick and sluggish.

He stared at his hands, barely able to focus on them now. They looked frozen in place, paralyzed.

His heart began to race. Again and again he tried to move his fingers but failed. Failed not only himself, but his fellow Stargate agents, and his country.

Nick held his breath like he always did. But no matter how often he'd seen this vision play out, he never looked away, always hoping against all hope that this time the outcome would be different. It wasn't.

The explosion on the screen was of massive proportions. The shockwave reached the water moments later, blasting the boats off their course and into the air, crushing them as if they were made of matchsticks. Bits of sail cloth flew like tiny birds in the churning air.

But by that time the shockwave had reached Nick, too, and he was flung in the air and catapulted toward the wall. For a split second before he hit it, he saw the house he'd been in: a mansion, though it wasn't his.

"Nooooo!"

His own scream pulled him from the vision. Bathed in sweat, he reared up. There was darkness all around him. He was in bed. Next to him, somebody moved.

"Nick?" It was the panicked voice of a woman.

Breathing hard, he tried to concentrate, tried to remember where he was. It took him three seconds to find his bearings.

"I'm fine," he said, already dragging his legs out of bed to sit up at the edge. "Just a bad dream. Go back to sleep, Michelle."

He felt her hand on his back and instinctively jerked away.

"But, you're—"

"I'm fine." He jumped up. "I'll take a shower if you don't mind, then I'll go."

Before Michelle could voice a protest, he left her bedroom and closed the door behind him. Outside in the hallway, he ran a shaky hand through his damp hair and tried to calm his pounding heart.

The vision, unlike all his other premonitions, came only during sleep and was becoming more frequent, as if to show him that the event he was seeing was coming closer. Yet he was no closer to averting it than he'd been three years ago when he'd first had this premonition after the murder of the founder of the top secret Stargate program.

He was running out of time.

# 12

Michelle stared at the closed bedroom door Nick had just disappeared through. She leaned over to her bedside table and switched on the lamp. Soft light illuminated the otherwise dark room. She glanced at the alarm clock. It was just after five in the morning.

Her heart still raced. She'd been sound asleep when Nick's scream had woken her. It had sounded as if he'd been in mortal danger and for an instant she'd wondered if somebody had broken into her apartment. But it was clear now that Nick had had a nightmare.

But why? What grown man had nightmares? It was the stuff kids dealt with, when they dreamed about monsters. Or maybe people who'd gone through some recent trauma. But Nick struck her as thoroughly balanced. But what if he wasn't? Had she made an error in judgment? What was wrong with the stranger she'd invited into her bed?

Heart beating in her throat, Michelle jumped out of bed and slipped on a T-shirt and a pair of yoga pants. When she entered the hallway, she heard the shower running. She flipped the light switch in the hallway. Careful not to make a sound, she looked around and quickly found what she was looking for.

Nick had dumped his backpack underneath the side table. Darting a look back to the closed bathroom door, Michelle crouched down and opened the zipper. She peered inside. One compartment held his laptop. She didn't pull it out, but instead looked through the rest.

There wasn't much: a set of keys, a cell phone with a charger, and a power cable for the laptop. She was about to close the bag again, when she felt a bulge. She opened the zipper as wide as she could, but there was nothing to see. However, there was clearly something there. She let her fingers do the searching, until she finally found a hidden zipper.

Glancing back at the bathroom door to assure herself that Nick was still in there, she took a deep breath and unzipped the hidden compartment. Holding her breath, she reached her hand inside.

Her fingers connected with something cold. She ran them along the metal item and felt its outline. Her heart stopped as her hand wrapped around the handle of a weapon. Slowly, carefully, she pulled it out. A handgun. She wasn't an expert, but she could tell it was a pistol with a magazine.

Her hand shook. The trembling spread to her entire body.

Fuck! What was Nick doing with a gun?

Fear suddenly gripping her, she shoved it back into the compartment and zipped it up again, then closed the backpack and placed it back where she'd found it.

Looking around, she tried to think what to do. Was Nick dangerous? Was he a criminal? Who the hell was he? Her eyes darted around and she looked back into her bedroom. There, over the back of a chair hung Nick's pants. He hadn't taken them into the bathroom with him.

She dashed into the bedroom and took the pants off the chair, searching the pockets. She pulled out his wallet. Casting a nervous look over her shoulder, she opened his wallet and examined the contents. Cash. A driver's license. She pulled it out, read it. The name was Nicholas Young, the address was in

Washington D.C. It had been issued two years earlier. Hadn't he said that he'd only just moved to Washington? How could he have a driver's license that was already two years old?

She looked through the remaining compartments of the wallet and felt something rigid. She dug her fingers into it and pulled out the item: a credit card. Her breath caught in her throat. Last night, he'd paid cash, claiming that his credit card had been stolen and he hadn't received a replacement card yet. Why would he say that, when clearly he had one? Was it an old one that had expired? She looked at the expiration date. No, it was still valid. Then her eyes darted to the left of it, where his name was embossed.

She slapped her hand over her mouth so she wouldn't scream. The name didn't match his driver's license. Marcus Tremont it said there.

*Shit!*

Shaking now, she shoved the wallet back into his pants pocket and ran into the living room. She pulled her computer from her bag and switched it on. While it booted up, she drummed her fingers on her thighs, continuously darting nervous looks back to the hallway. But the water in the shower kept running.

The moment her computer was on, she unlocked the screen with her password and pulled up a browser. She first searched for Nicholas Young. There were too many hits. The name was too common. Even an actor and a baseball star were among the search result. She would need time to go through them all.

*Damn!*

She typed in Marcus Tremont instead. There was only one Marcus Tremont. She clicked on the Facebook link. The profile picture was blank and there were no posts in his timeline, none she could see without being his friend anyway.

Who was Nick? And why was he here?

The answer hit her in the face like a closing door. Smith! Her *Deep-Throat-like* handler had to be behind it. Had he sensed that she was getting desperate to make a run for it? Did he already realize that she was preparing for her escape and wanted to make sure she didn't get away before she'd delivered what he wanted?

Why hadn't she thought of this earlier? He must have had tabs on her all along, having her watched every moment just in case she didn't comply with his demands. How stupid had she been! Nick running into her at the coffee shop and then, later, when she'd nearly stepped in the path of the taxi couldn't be a coincidence. Smith had set it up. And for all she knew, he'd even orchestrated it so that the taxi would almost hit her so Nick could save her and thus gain her confidence.

And she'd fallen for that cheap trick. Hadn't she seen this kind of thing happening countless times in movies and TV shows? She should have recognized it for what it was: a ploy. A trick for Nick to get close so he could watch her, maybe even gain her trust so she would tell him what she was planning.

She wanted to curse, to scream, but she couldn't. She had to play along now, not let him know that she knew, that she'd discovered his deception and was onto him. She had to remain calm and behave as if nothing had happened.

The door of the bathroom opening nearly made her jump out of her skin.

*Way to go,* Michelle, she chastised herself silently. *That'll look normal.*

Nick didn't come into the living room, but headed straight for the bedroom. She heard him get dressed. She used the little time it bought her to take deep breaths and calm herself. When she heard his footsteps again, she quickly slammed the lid of her laptop shut and stood up.

"Michelle." His voice was hesitant.

Slowly, she turned, facing him. She tried a smile but failed.

"Sorry, I, uh... didn't mean to frighten you earlier." He ran a hand through his damp hair, looking utterly crushed. "The nightmares, they've become less frequent."

"Nightmares?" she echoed.

"Yeah. I was in Iraq. It was hell." He dropped his gaze to his feet.

"Iraq? You were in the war?" Did that explain at least his nightmares? It could. And oddly enough it could also explain other things. If he was ex-military, then it made even more sense that Smith had hired him to keep tabs on her.

"Yeah. One tour, but it was enough." He paused. "Listen, I'd better go. I've got work to do. I'll call you tonight?"

She nodded quickly, eager for him to leave her apartment. When he walked up to her instead, she tensed. He froze a foot away from her, clearly having noticed her apprehension.

"I'm sorry again, I know it must have scared you." He leaned in and pressed a kiss to her cheek.

"It's okay." Michelle forced a smile.

"Talk later, okay?"

Nick turned and walked to the door, grabbing his backpack on the way out. Only when the door snapped shut behind him was she able to breathe again.

"Oh God," she murmured to herself. "I've slept with the enemy."

# 13

Nick pulled his laptop from its compartment and placed it on his desk, before he tossed the backpack in the corner, angry at himself.

He was used to lying to cover his ass, but by God, he'd hated lying to Michelle, telling her he was an Iraq vet suffering from post traumatic stress. What a cheap shot that had been. There were lots of real Iraq vets out there dealing with PTSD and worse. And there he was, using them to cover up his real issues.

He'd never served in the military, though he'd served his country as a CIA agent for many years. He'd sacrificed his life to keep the people of this country safe, and how had they repaid him? By chasing him down like a dog. It was time to fight back.

But first things first.

Nick navigated to the folder where he'd saved the information from Michelle's flash drive and looked at the files. One was a picture file. He clicked it open. It was a portrait of Michelle. He recognized immediately what it was for, the lack of a smile and the way her head was turned, giving away its purpose. It was a passport picture. Only, why would she have a digital version of it? Passport pictures were normally submitted in printed form when applying through the post office.

Curious, Nick perused the other files.

One was a resume. He scanned it quickly. There wasn't much. A few jobs as a software consultant and a degree from an online university, as well as a list of computer programs Michelle was proficient in: C, Fortran, JavaScript, Lisp, Python. She clearly knew her stuff.

Nick closed the document and continued. A small text file drew his attention. He opened it and read the two lines of information: Jennifer Miller, birth date: May 5, 1991, hair: dark blond, eyes: blue, height: 5'7". All information needed for a passport, though the name didn't match. Was Michelle Andrews trying to become Jennifer Miller? To what purpose? He opened the next text file. It only contained one item: an email address.

Nick logged into one of his bogus email accounts and drafted a message, leaving the text blank and only putting one word into the subject line: *Inquiry*. He pressed *Send* and waited. Sixty seconds later, his email account pinged. The message landing in his inbox was from *System Administrator*, and the subject line said *Undeliverable*. The text stated that the email address didn't exist. Just as he'd suspected. Whoever had used this email address had already deactivated it.

"What are you up to, Michelle?" he murmured.

He opened document after document. Job applications and documents with hyperlinks. He followed the links and reviewed them in his browser: research on different countries, one leading directly to a PDF document. He flew over the text, wondering what she was looking for, when one word stuck out: *Extradition*. He read the sentence. *There is no extradition treaty in place with the U.S.*

It was clear now: Michelle was running from the law.

He tried to piece together what he knew about her so far: a past with Anonymous that could have gotten her into trouble with the authorities; electronic files that could be used to get a fake passport; a bogus email address that most likely put her in touch with a person who could procure such a passport; research on countries that didn't extradite criminals back to the US; and

Michelle being the prime suspect for trying to keep him out of the CIA's servers. It all fit. Somebody who knew about her past had to have hired her. Had that person offered her a large sum of money, maybe even provided the contact to get a fake passport so she could start a life far away from here?

Or was somebody using her past against her, forcing her to flush him out, and she was doing this against her will? Either scenario was possible. In any case, it meant he couldn't trust Michelle, though he'd already known that from the start. The information he'd uncovered from her flash drive only cemented what he'd already suspected: that she was trying to get the drop on him. But he was smarter.

Just as he was opening the next document from Michelle's drive, an alert pinged in his inbox. He switched screens and read it.

Finally.

The notification was from an advertisement he'd placed on the Dark Web. He logged off his current internet connection. From his desk drawer he retrieved a pre-paid jetpack and jammed it into one of the slots in his laptop, then connected to the web from there. He would dispose of the jetpack to ensure his IP address remained secret after he was done so nobody would be able to trace him to his current location.

It took only moments until he was in the right place on the Dark Web to retrieve the message that had been sent to him. There was no sender's name. But the message itself was compelling. Somebody had seen his meeting request and wanted to set up a time and place. All keywords the person used were the right ones. Keywords the members of Stargate used. While some of them could of course be used by anybody, the fact that all of them were in the message pointed to the conclusion that the person who was contacting him was a fellow Stargate agent.

Still, Nick knew to be careful. There was always a chance that an enemy was coercing a Stargate agent to reveal his secrets by whatever means necessary. Not even a Stargate agent was immune to torture. Therefore, he'd take all necessary precautions before he set the meet. He wouldn't go in unarmed.

But he had to go. He couldn't let this opportunity go by. For too long he'd been searching for his fellow agents so he could finally unravel the mystery in his darkest premonition. He needed to stop whatever was going to happen. It was big. He knew that instinctively, bigger than what he could handle himself.

He needed help.

Help only another trusted Stargate agent could provide. It was worth the risk.

# 14

The message had been clear. Michelle was to go to a specific spot in Constitution Gardens tonight and record what she saw. There would be a clandestine meeting. If she performed well, Smith had texted her, maybe she'd even be rewarded for it. Michelle scoffed at that. What kind of reward was Smith thinking of? To kill her quickly should the people who were meeting clandestinely in some deserted corner of Washington discover her and try to torture her to tell them what she knew—which was nothing—so she wouldn't have to suffer?

Great. It was bad enough that she had to spy on some hacker online, now Smith actively put her in harm's way by sending her out on a nightly mission. Hell, she wasn't trained for this. Why didn't he use one of his covert agents—which he surely had, Nick being one of them!—or do the dirty job himself? No, he had to use a weak woman for that, one who didn't even know karate or any other form of self-defense. A fat chance in hell—that's all she'd have when it came to survival.

Damn it.

In her hiding place, behind a bush, she kept quiet though she wanted to scream at the injustice of it all. Wasn't it enough that Smith had assigned her a watcher?

Michelle had arrived under cover of darkness only moments after the sun had gone down and it was dark enough so nobody would notice her creeping around and get suspicious. Hours before the presumed meeting was to take place, she was already waiting, poised to record whatever she saw.

Meanwhile, the mosquitoes swirled around her, eating her alive. It hadn't cooled down despite the thunderstorm the night before. In her black, long-sleeved T-shirt and her dark pants, she felt too hot and woefully overdressed, though it meant that the mosquitoes only caught her hands, neck, and face, although she could swear that some were trying to work their way up her pant leg. She slapped at her lower leg, where she felt the sting, and cursed under her breath.

*Bloodsuckers!*

There were still tourists around, taking pictures of the various monuments in the park, which were lit up by strong spotlights. Lincoln Memorial, of which she had a good view across the Reflecting Pool, was one of them. People were taking pictures on the stairs, selfies with the sitting statue of President Lincoln behind them, or group photos, asking other tourists for help. But the longer she waited, the less people she saw. The tourists finally withdrew, returning to their hotels or other, more interesting sights by night.

Michelle crouched between the bushes, looking around herself. She didn't want to miss the arrival of the mysterious strangers or be spotted by them.

The silence in the large park was eerie. There was the sound of birds fluttering in the dark, and the annoying buzzing of some overeager flies and mosquitoes, but all human-made sounds were in the distance. Cars driving on Constitution and Independence Avenues, others crossing Arlington Memorial Bridge. In the dark, the sounds carried far. But they were also soothing, almost comforting, because they confirmed that normal life continued—while her life was taking a turn for the worse. She knew it. She could sense it in her bones, feel it by the way the hairs at her nape stood up as if to protest.

She shouldn't be here. She should be on a plane to South America, fake passport in hand. But she was still waiting for that fake passport. Her contact—recommended by an old friend from Anonymous—had urged her to be patient. If the passport needed to pass federal inspection at a US airport, it needed to be perfect. He couldn't rush it, but he'd promised to deliver it in two days, just before her ultimatum with the mysterious Mr. Smith ran out. She would be out of here before he could throw her into prison. And he would, given half a chance, because the hacker she'd been so close to nailing, had gone dark. The entire week, she'd not seen his digital signature anywhere. As if he knew she was onto him.

The sound of a twig breaking shattered the silence and made her snap her head in the other direction. She tried to adjust her eyes, searching in the dark for the person who'd created that sound, but saw nothing. The area it had come from was too dark—not lit up like the monuments around her. She would need night-vision goggles. Smith should have thought of that. Clearly, her blackmailer wasn't quite as smart as he pretended to be. How was she going to see anything, and know what to record? Hell, her cell phone wouldn't be able to pick up anything if she didn't even know which direction to point it in.

There, another sound! This time, it was clearly footsteps. Their echo was difficult to pinpoint. Was the sound coming from the right or the left? She shifted, and her T-shirt got snagged on a branch. She jerked back. The ripping sound resonated in the silence.

*Shit!*

~ ~ ~

The person hiding in the bushes was no Stargate agent, Nick assessed immediately. He was close enough that he would have been able to sense the special aura a Stargate member gave off. It was something he'd discovered early on after he'd been recruited by Henry Sheppard. He'd instantly felt a kindred spirit with the older man, as if he'd known him a long time.

Sheppard had told him that it was like recognizing like. One Stargate agent recognizing another. It was a survival instinct. Nature had made sure that some of its special children knew each other and could come to each other's aid should it be necessary.

Nick had no illusions that the person hiding in the darkness meant him harm and wasn't just a lost tourist. He recognized that the stranger was holding his breath, trying not to be heard. But he couldn't see his would-be assailant, because the area was pitch-black, while only a few yards away there was sufficient light from the monuments and the city itself to see outlines and shapes.

Not knowing what training the person lying in wait had, Nick took no chances. One wrong move and he could have a bullet in his brain or a knife in his heart. And he was rather fond of his life and not ready to trade it in for an eternal sojourn in a wooden box six feet under.

Nick had undergone basic CIA training at The Farm, training that encompassed self-defense, hand-to-hand combat, and weaponry, even before he'd been recruited into the Stargate program by Sheppard. He'd been selected by a CIA recruiter for his computer skills right out of college and assigned to data security at Langley a full two years before Henry Sheppard had taken notice of him. Even after being drafted in the Stargate program, he'd continued to work at Langley in his less secret capacity as a data security analyst.

Nick had become particularly fond of his Glock, a handgun that handled well and was currently holstered under his left arm, ready to be deployed at a moment's notice.

Setting one foot in front of the other, treading lightly so as not to make any sounds, Nick stalked toward the copse of trees and bushes. He circled to the left, slowly approaching. His breathing was even and silent, his eyes trained on the target in front of him. While night-vision goggles would have come in handy and given him a definite advantage, he knew he could make up for this lack of equipment with his other senses—including his impeccable sharpshooting skills.

Calmly, he reached into his jacket and pulled the Glock from its holster. A few more steps. He was close.

A rustle in the bushes as if the assailant was moving, shifting, sensing that he'd been discovered.

But it was too late. Nick was already onto him. Behind him. Only a few feet now. Nick lifted his leg, set it down a foot ahead of him. He felt the twig beneath his sole too late and cracked it. The sound echoed in the night.

A sharp intake of air was the response, then a sudden movement right in front of him: the stranger spinning around to face him. He wasn't tall for a man, average in fact, and lightly built.

Nick lunged forward, slamming the man into the tree. A split second later, he pressed the Glock's cold barrel to the would-be assailant's forehead, cocking it.

"One wrong move, and this bullet will make mush out of your brain."

A loud gasp, the sound too high-pitched to come from a man, startled him for a second. Just as the uncontrollable trembling did.

"Nick! Don't!"

Shock charged through his bones, paralyzing him for an instant. But then his training kicked in.

"Michelle!" he ground out. He hadn't expected her, though he should have.

"Oh God, thank you," she let out, seemingly relieved. "Please, take that gun away. You're scaring me."

"Am I?" It could all be a ploy to get him to lower his gun so she could take him out. He moved closer. "Are you armed?"

"Armed? No!"

He used his free hand to frisk her, first her front, then he reached behind her to check if she'd tucked a gun into the back of her jeans. She hadn't.

"What are you doing?" Panic laced her voice. "Nick, tell me what's going on!"

"I was gonna ask you the same question." He moved closer now, close enough so he could make out her facial features.

Yeah, it was definitely Michelle, dressed all in black like a ninja, her dark blond hair hidden under a scarf she'd tied at her nape. At least she hadn't blackened her cheeks with shoe polish.

"I was just, uh, you know, going for a walk," she mumbled.

He pressed her harder against the tree trunk. "Try again, *honey!*"

She pulled her shoulders down, puffing up her chest. "I swear! I was just minding my own business, and then I heard something, so I figured, I'd hide. You know, there are muggers in the park at night."

He scoffed. "Yeah, right. Then why the fuck would you take a walk in a dark park at night when it's so dangerous, huh? Care to explain that?"

"Well, then what are you doing here? Spying on me?"

"Don't try to turn the tables on me. We both know what's going on here. You set me up to come to the park."

"To do what?" she spat, defiance spewing from those lips he'd devoured the night before.

"To kill me," he ground out, shoving his face practically into hers. Her blue eyes sparkled now, picking up light from somewhere in the vicinity as she glared at him.

Michelle gnashed her teeth. "With what, you idiot? Maybe with the gun you're still pointing at my head?"

He had to give her that: she wasn't caving easily, more proof that she was smart and out to trick him.

"Now get off me!" She tried to push him, but he was heavier and stronger, and had no intention of relinquishing his superior position just because she was a woman.

"Not until you tell me what you're doing here. Were you the one setting up the meet?"

"What meet?"

The way her eyes shifted at her words, he knew she was covering, buying herself some time to get out of her predicament.

"You know what meet." He looked her up and down. "Of course it was you, wasn't it? Who else would know how to navigate the Deep Web but a former member of Anonymous?"

Her chin dropped and air rushed from her lungs. She tried to catch herself, but it was too late; she'd already given herself away.

"I don't know what you're talking about."

"Don't you?" With his free hand, he reached for her necklace and pulled on it, until the pendant emerged from underneath her black long-sleeved T-shirt. "Odd choice for a piece of jewelry, don't you think?"

Her eyes narrowed. "I can wear what I like."

"Sure you can. And I can draw whatever conclusions from it that I like. And that, *my sweet*, is a Guy Fawkes mask, the symbol of Anonymous. Which you were a member of. What happened? The authorities catch you when you were a hacker?"

"I was never a hacker! And you have no right to question me. You're the one who's got something to hide, not I." She motioned to the gun he was still pointing at her head. "You're the one with the gun, remember?"

"And that is exactly the reason why you should be answering my questions truthfully and not dishing up any more lies. I'm growing impatient, Michelle, and you know what happens when I get impatient?"

She stared at him quizzically.

"My hand starts to tremble. It's a little tick, you know."

"You wouldn't."

He shook his head. Michelle had courage, the kind of courage that could get her killed one day. "Don't test me. Tell me the truth, Michelle, or would you rather I guessed what you're up to?"

"Be my guest!"

"Well, then." He loosened his hold on her by a bit while he lowered the barrel to her neck. "You were a hacker associated with Anonymous. You got caught at some point, hacking into some government agency or another. You're talented. So talented in fact that they made you an offer: to work for them. How am I doing so far?"

She pressed her lips together.

"Good. I'm on the right track then. Shall I continue, or would you rather take over and tell me the rest?"

"There's nothing to tell."

He slammed his fist into the tree trunk next to her head. She flinched.

"Goddamn it, Michelle, I swear I'm going to strangle you if don't drop your stubbornness and tell me what I want to know. Don't you get it? This is not a game. Lives are at stake here." He moved in, bringing his face to hover only inches from hers. "Were you the one to set up the meet?"

She shook her head, trembling now. "I was told to record whoever was showing up here." Tears brimmed at her eyes. "I didn't know it was going to be you."

He breathed a sigh of relief. Finally, Michelle was talking. Softening his voice, he asked, "The person you work for, who is he with? CIA? NSA?"

She gave a helpless shrug. "I don't know."

Nick growled. "Michelle."

"I swear I don't know." She sucked in a breath. "I don't know who he is. He contacts me and tells me what to do. I have no choice."

He studied her face for a moment, wheels clicking into place now. "His offer to work for him wasn't really an offer, was it?"

Silently, she shook her head and dropped her lids.

"Is that why you're getting a fake passport made?"

Her head shot up and she pinned him with her eyes. "How do you know that?"

"The flash drive on your key ring. You had image files and information on it that pointed to it."

She braced her hands at her hips, suddenly furious. "You took my memory stick? That's private property. You had no right!"

He shrugged. Private property rights weren't really his concern right now. He had bigger fish to fry. "Should have encrypted it."

"There's no need to encrypt it! It never leaves my sight."

He pasted a grin on his face. "It did when you took a shower."

"You, you…" Her hands came up as if she wanted to hit him, but he stopped her by pressing the gun harder against her neck.

Her eyes darted to it. "Don't you think that's a little overkill right now? You've assured yourself already that I'm not armed. Or do you use that gun as an extension of your dick?"

He chuckled involuntarily. He couldn't really blame her for being angry; neither could he take that kind of insult lying down. "My dick needs no extension, as you well know."

She huffed indignantly.

But she'd made her point, and knowing what he knew of her so far, Michelle posed no physical threat to him. He put the safety back on the gun and holstered it, but didn't step back, keeping her trapped between his body and the tree trunk.

"Now that we've established the size of my dick, let's continue. What else did your mysterious handler want you to do?"

"Just record the people who were going to meet here and then text him the file."

"I don't mean tonight. I mean in general. You were stalking me online, trying to prevent me from hacking into a server."

Her mouth gaped open for a second, before she spoke. "So that was you."

"Yeah, that was me. You're pretty good, but you made a mistake."

"How?"

"Doesn't matter. I traced your IP address to the coffee shop."

She nodded. "So it wasn't a coincidence then. Too good to be true. You played me all this time. Got into my pants just so you could figure me out, that it?" She tossed him an angry glare.

"And trust me, I enjoyed it, and so did you."

"Jerk! I would have never slept with you had I known—"

He pressed his body to hers, grinding his hips into her pelvis, snatching her wrists with both his hands, and pinning her against the tree.

"You don't know anything, Michelle. Or do you know how I fought with my conscience whether to seduce you or not? Whether to take you to bed or not? How I agonized over it, knowing that it was wrong to touch you when I knew I was doing it to get information from you?"

He lowered his lids, only looking at her parted lips now.

"While all this time, I wanted you, wanted to be with you and make love to you as if we were normal people who are attracted to each other. Do you know that I wished that my suspicions were wrong? That you weren't the hacker they'd sent to catch me?"

He released her wrists and shoved a hand through his hair, realizing something for the first time.

"Damn it, I slept with you because I wanted you. I could have gotten the information I needed by other means, too. By breaking into your place, or by mugging you. I didn't need to get this close. But I wanted to."

Just like he wanted her now beyond all reason.

Unable to stop himself, he sank his lips onto hers, taking her mouth in a fierce kiss.

# 15

Nick's unexpected kiss robbed her of her breath. All Michelle could do now was cling to him. Her knees were too weak to support her weight, and only the tree at her back and Nick's body pressing into her were holding her up. She had no strength left, no fight left in her. Nick holding the gun to her head and having looked like he was actually going to use it had squashed any kind of resistance she'd tried to mount. She'd been surprised at herself that she'd held out as long as she had. But no longer. Because resisting Nick's kiss was impossible.

His words continued to swarm in her head, bouncing around like ricochets, urging her to believe what he'd said. That he hadn't wanted to use her. That he could have done it without sleeping with her. That he'd only slept with her because he'd wanted her.

She shouldn't believe it. No. She *couldn't*. He was only saying this to gain her trust so she would tell him everything. He knew too much already. But the way he acted made no sense. If he worked for Smith, why was he asking her all these things? He would already know that she was beholden to Smith. Or was she wrong? Was he in fact *not* one of Smith's pawns? Was he truly who he said he was, the hacker she'd been charged to find?

She pushed him away, making him release her lips. Resisting the urge to rub her fingers over her mouth to verify that he'd truly kissed her with such passion, she glared at him instead. She needed answers.

"Are you saying you're not working for Smith? That he didn't send you to check up on me? To keep me in line?"

"Smith?"

"The guy who's making me do all this."

"Why would you think that?"

"Because it's just a little too convenient that you showed up just after he gave me an ultimatum."

Nick grabbed her shoulders. "What ultimatum?"

"If I don't deliver the hacker to him in ten days, he'll throw my ass in jail, though I think he didn't mean it. I think he plans to kill me because he's afraid I know too much."

"When did he give you the ultimatum?"

"A week ago yesterday."

"That leaves you two days."

Michelle swallowed hard. She could count, too. She knew her time was nearly up. "He said if I did well tonight, then, maybe, he'd let me off the hook." She snorted. "Like that's ever gonna happen now." She pushed back the tears of desperation that threatened to turn her into a pitiful mess and looked at him. "You've gotta let me go. I don't care what you're involved in. I don't even want to know. But I need to get out of here."

"You really think he's not gonna find out what you're planning? Don't you think he already knows that you're trying to procure a fake passport and are planning your getaway to South America?"

For a moment, she froze. How did he know about South America? Then it clicked. "The flash drive. It was on there, my research."

Nick nodded, his face a mask of seriousness now. "I think we can help each other."

She shook her head and her torso, trying to shake off his hands, but he held firm. "Yeah, that's how he put it, too. And look what happened. I'm in a deeper mess than I ever was before. Why would I trade in one blackmailer for another? How's that gonna help me?"

"I'll make sure you stay alive. I can protect you against Smith. If you help me."

"Do what? Don't you get it, Nick? You're the better hacker. You traced my digital signature. *You* found *me*. That wasn't supposed to happen. So how could I possibly help you when you're so much better than me?"

"It's not about that. It's about who you know. Smith. I need to get to him. If he knew that I was trying to get into the CIA's servers, then he also knows why. And that means he knows what I am."

Confused, Michelle shook her head. "Then why would he need me to find out? That makes no sense."

"It makes perfect sense," Nick shot back. "Because he knows *what* I am, but not *who* I am."

"I don't understand."

"You don't need to. All you need to know is that, if you tell me where I can find Smith, I'll help you disappear."

She shook her head in disbelief. "And how would you know anything about how to disappear?"

His head came closer, until all she could see were his penetrating eyes. "I disappeared three years ago. None of my enemies has been able to find me. And I'm right under their noses."

"Enemies? Like Smith? Is he your enemy?"

"If he's looking for me, most likely."

Curiosity got the better of her, even though she'd told herself and Nick only moments earlier that she didn't want to know what he was involved in. "What did you do?"

"It doesn't matter."

But she couldn't let it go. "Smith is government, I know that much, though I'm not sure what agency. Probably CIA. That means you did something the government didn't like. Espionage? Treason?"

Nick chuckled unexpectedly. "Those are mighty words for an anarchist like yourself."

"I'm not an anarchist. I believe in democracy. All I ever did was expose corruption and wrongdoing in the government."

"By hacking into classified information together with your friends at Anonymous, I suppose?"

"Look who's calling the kettle black. Besides, Anonymous is doing good things, too. They've pledged to shut down Al-Qaeda's online presence."

A smile formed on Nick's lips. "I'm not defending the government, Michelle, so you can stop your tirade. We're on the same side, or at least I hope I'm able to convince you to come to my side. You need me."

She contemplated his words, falling silent for a good long moment. Could he really deliver what he was promising? A new start, somewhere nobody could find her? Where she was safe from Smith and whatever government agency he worked for?

"You know you want to say yes. Let me make the decision easier for you."

She raised an eyebrow, wondering what he was planning, when his hand came up to caress her cheek.

"I won't hurt you, Michelle. I'll protect you. Trust me."

"Trust isn't a thing you can force."

"But it's something that can grow. You trusted me with your body, now trust me with your heart and your mind."

Slowly his lips approached her mouth. His breath whispered over her skin, tempting her to surrender, to give herself over to this man, this stranger who'd taken her body to unknown heights. At the same time, he'd lied to her. How could she trust him now?

"Nick, please..." She didn't know what she wanted to tell or ask him, didn't know why her fingers suddenly clawed into his shirt, holding him close.

"Baby, just let me help you. Let me keep you safe."

His lips brushed against hers so gently that she wasn't even sure he was touching her. Only when the pressure against her mouth intensified and a hot tongue swept over her trembling lips, did her resistance crumble.

"I'm not your enemy," he murmured against her lips and dipped his tongue between them.

The clicking of a gun paralyzed her and made Nick spin around in her arms.

"Wow, you sure are a smooth operator," a male voice drawled. "Guess even I can learn something from you."

# 16

Hand on his gun, Nick froze. The man standing only a few feet away, pointing a gun at him, caused the small hairs on his skin to stand to attention. A familiar tingling spread over his body, and he recognized it instantly. He was facing another Stargate agent. This wasn't the mysterious Mr. Smith Michelle had told him about, or at least he hoped not. Only Michelle could confirm.

"Leave that gun right where it is," the man ordered.

Nick turned his head sideways, without taking his eyes off the stranger. Tall and athletic-looking, the man appeared to be in his early thirties, his dark blond hair hanging over his forehead, yet cut short on the sides. He was clean shaven and appeared well groomed. "Michelle, is this him? Is this Smith?"

She peered past him. "It's not his voice."

"What?" Did that mean what he thought it meant?

"I've never seen him. I only know his voice."

The stranger clicked his tongue. "You shouldn't have let me get the drop on you. Getting sloppy, my man."

The fact that the man addressed him as if they knew each other unnerved Nick, but he pretended that he didn't mind. "You're late," Nick said instead.

"Actually, I was early." He motioned to Michelle, who was now trying to squeeze past him. Nick pushed her behind his back. "Just like this one here showed up early. I was wondering what she was planning."

"We need to talk," Nick said firmly. Preferably without the other Stargate member pointing a gun at his head. Clearly the man had trust issues, and while Nick had been close to wiping out Michelle's reluctance to trust him with seduction, the same method wasn't going to work on his fellow Stargate agent.

Not that he could blame the guy. Nick himself wasn't sure whether he could trust him either. Sheppard had warned them that should the program ever be compromised they'd have to assume the worst: that one of their own was a traitor. That one of their own could come to hunt them down, using the very skill that had made them brothers against them.

"Yeah. Alone," the stranger responded. "Lock her up."

"No!" Michelle protested, her head darting past Nick's shoulder.

The stranger's gun veered toward her. "You don't have a say in this."

"But I do," Nick countered, glaring at the man.

"Unarmed, you don't."

"You know I'm not unarmed."

The man cocked his head to the side. "And just how fast a draw are you?" He made a small movement with this gun. "It takes way less time to pull the trigger with the finger already on it. So don't be stupid." He motioned to a path beyond the copse of trees. "There's a shed down there, a couple hundred yards away. She'll be fine in there while we talk."

Nick glanced at Michelle, seeking eye contact. She stared back at him, frightened. "I won't let anything happen to you."

Why he felt he had to make her that promise, a promise he was determined to keep, he wasn't entirely sure, particularly since at this moment he wasn't in the position to make promises—not with a gun pointed at his head.

Michelle pressed her lips together and swallowed.

"Walk."

Nick reached for Michelle's hand and followed the stranger's order. The time it took to reach the storage shed tucked away between some trees seemed to take forever. During the entire time, Nick went through various scenarios of how to turn the tables on the guy following them. But every scenario meant putting Michelle's life in danger. It was better to take a wait-and-see approach, until he could figure out whether the guy was friend or foe. At least, Nick would be alone with him at that point, which would mean he'd only have to worry about his own life.

The lock on the shed was perfunctory at best and gave way easily.

Nick urged Michelle into the dark interior, noticing her shiver at the prospect of being locked up.

"Take her phone," the stranger ordered.

Nick stretched his hand out, nodding to Michelle to follow the barked command. She dug into her pocket and pulled it out, placing it in his palm.

"I'll be back soon. Trust me."

She lifted her eyes to his then, staring long and hard at him. "I hope I won't regret this."

So did he. With a last look at her, he closed the shed door, when his fellow Stargate agent handed him a chain.

"Loop it through the handle and that hook, then tie it."

Nick did as he was told. When it was done, he turned back to the man.

"This way."

They walked to a small hedge, where the guy stopped. "This'll do. She won't be able to hear us here."

Nick stopped and pivoted, watching to his surprise how the man holstered his gun and adopted a more relaxed stance.

"Name's Yankee."

"Fox." Suspiciously, Nick glanced at the gun now on Yankee's hip. "What changed your mind about me?"

"Overheard you talking to that woman for quite a while. Told me enough to know you're clean." He motioned to the shed. "Doesn't mean I was gonna reveal who I am in front of her. Neither should you. Can't trust anybody. Nice attempt though with her. She might play ball if we're lucky."

He ignored Yankee's last comments and asked instead, "And how am I gonna know whether you haven't turned against Stargate?"

"'Cause I'm telling you."

"Not good enough."

"You're still alive. Could have shot you a hundred times over and you wouldn't have known what hit you."

Nick couldn't argue with that, though that didn't mean he liked the guy's modus operandi. "Enjoy that macho stuff much?"

Yankee grinned from one ear to the other, looking overly smug. "It gets the job done."

"Don't think Michelle appreciated it much," Nick said dryly.

"I'm not really concerned with what a civilian is thinking. I've got more important things on my mind."

"Which would be?"

"The Stargate agents are under attack."

"No shit. You're only catching onto that now? Where were you three years ago?"

"In the same situation as you: running for my life. I'm sick of running and hiding. It's time to act."

"Why now?"

"Because the shit just hit the fan." Yankee glanced around, listening, looking, before turning his face back to Nick. "Echo is dead."

Though he didn't know the person Yankee was referring to, Nick assumed the name was a code name. "A Stargate agent?"

Yankee nodded, a sad expression on his face. "He'd gone bad. Worked for our enemies. By the time he changed his mind and wanted to make good, it was already too late. But what's done is done. Can't wallow in the past. I know something big is coming. Something real bad."

"What is it?" Nick asked, drawing in closer, curious now.

"You have the dream, too? The dream about the inferno, the destruction?"

Shocked, Nick stumbled back a few paces, his mouth gaping. How could Yankee know about the horrific premonition that haunted his sleep?

Yankee nodded to himself. "So you do. Echo had it, too. That's why I figured all of us have that same dream." He shoved a hand through his hair. "Anyway, after talking to Echo before he died, I realized that we see slightly different parts of that premonition, and it made me think that maybe others do, too. If we have all of the parts, maybe if we piece them together something might start making sense. That's why I started looking for others from the program."

"So what do you want from me?"

"Same you want from me. Resurrect Stargate, let us rise once more. That's why you put your feelers out there on the Dark Web for one of us to find you, isn't it? I'm here, and I'm ready to fight." Yankee put his hand on his holster to underscore his words.

"It's not that easy. This isn't gonna be a shootout at the OK Corral, buddy. I'm working a different angle." Nick looked his fellow Stargate agent up and down, still unsure whether to trust him fully, though the fact that he was still alive—as was Michelle—was one point in Yankee's favor.

"As long as it'll take us to the same goal, I don't care much which way we're gonna play it." Yankee motioned toward the Lincoln Memorial. "Then let's go. We need to come up with a plan of action." He already turned and took a few steps.

"I'm not leaving Michelle here."

Yankee stopped and looked over his shoulder. "You'll have to. She can't come with us. She's a civilian, and she knows too much already. She's gonna lead our enemy right to us."

Nick squared his stance and fisted his hands at his sides. "I won't leave her. And that's final. We need her. She has information that's critical to what I'm planning."

"She's got pretty tits and a hot ass, that's all."

"Fucking asshole!" Nick growled and marched toward him.

"She's got no information. She admitted it herself. She's never seen that guy, that Smith. She won't be able to help us identify him, so put your dick back in your pants. Just because you've got the hots for her doesn't mean I'm gonna let her come."

Nick lunged at the guy and landed a blow in his face. His fellow Stargate agent lost no time in punching back, knocking Nick's head sideways.

When Nick pulled his fist back for another hook, Yankee growled, "Damn it, Fox, why didn't you say she was your girl?"

Nick froze in mid-movement.

"She is your girl, isn't she? It's just... from the things I overheard earlier, I couldn't really tell. Apologies."

Slowly, Nick relaxed and dropped his fist. Apparently he'd just given away something to his fellow Stargate agent that he hadn't realized himself yet: he didn't just have the hots for Michelle. He cared about her wellbeing, cared about *her*.

Without a word, Nick turned and walked toward the shed.

# 17

"Ouch!"

Michelle cursed as her hand slipped from the shovel's handle and another fingernail broke at her attempt to pry the door off the rickety shed. If she continued like this, she soon wouldn't have any fingernails left.

But she couldn't stop. She had to get out of here. What if that stranger was going to kill Nick? And once Nick was dead, the guy would take care of her. She shivered despite the muggy night air, and not only because she was in fear of her own life. To her surprise, she also worried about Nick, even though she shouldn't. He really didn't deserve it.

He'd insinuated himself in her life with lies. She didn't know what to believe anymore. Unfortunately that didn't stop her from caring about what happened to him. She'd spent a wonderful night with him and experienced a closeness to him that she hadn't felt with any other man before.

*It's only sex*, a voice in her head cautioned her. Was that true? Maybe. Then why was her heart contracting in pain when she imagined Nick lying on the ground, a bullet in his head? She tried to shake off the image. She couldn't let that happen. Somehow she had to help him. She wanted to believe that he would do the same for her in the same situation, though she had no idea if he would really risk his life for her.

However, there had been that brief moment when the gunman had shown up, when Nick had shielded her with his broad back, almost as if it had been an automatic reaction. A protector instinct that had kicked in. Because she was a woman? Or because she was the woman he'd slept with the night before? If only she knew.

His words still echoed in her mind.

*I didn't need to get this close. But I wanted to.*

Was it the truth? She was inclined to believe it, not because she was a hopeless romantic—which she was—but because Nick clearly had the skills to get to the information he wanted without sleeping with her. Hell, he'd managed to steal her flash drive *and* return it without her noticing, because, yes, she'd checked her key ring the moment they'd thrown her into the shed. And the flash drive dangled from it as if it had never been gone.

Nick could have easily broken into her apartment while she slept and taken what he needed. There'd been no need to even make her acquaintance. Had that been his plan at the beginning?

"Doesn't matter," she muttered to herself.

Being in Nick's arms had felt right. And now he'd offered her a way out of her current predicament, and—goddamn it—she wanted to accept his offer and believe that he could deliver what he promised. But for that to happen Nick had to stay alive. She could always kick his lying ass later and tell him what she thought of him.

The sound of a rattling chain tore her from her musings.

*Shit! Shit! Shit!*

Panic rose from her stomach to her throat, sending her heart racing and making her breath stutter to a halt. She gripped the shovel's wooden handle more tightly, holding onto it with both hands now, raising it for leverage.

Somebody pulled on the chain. The door moved back and forth on its hinges for a moment, before opening outward.

"There we go."

It was the voice of the stranger.

Without another thought, Michelle took two steps forward, clearing the door frame, before she swung at the dark figure waiting there for her.

"Shit, no, Michelle!"

Nick's outcry came in mid-swing, too late to pull back the shovel and divert its path. The dark figure—the stranger—lunged to the side, avoiding a hit to his head, but a second person—Nick—stood beside him. As the shovel completed its arc it landed right on Nick's ass, sending him flying into the dirt.

Nick grunted.

She dropped the shovel and was already running to him, crouching down next to him.

"Fuck, Michelle, what did you do that for?"

"Oh my God, did I hurt you?"

A belly laugh from the stranger made her whirl around.

"I think you guys have some real relationship issues you've gotta work on," the stranger said.

"I was aiming at you," she ground out.

"Maybe you wanna teach her some target practice, buddy."

Groaning, Nick pushed himself up to stand and reached for her, pulling her up, looking past her to the other man. "I blame you for that hit, not her. If you hadn't insisted on locking her into a shed full of gardening tools, that wouldn't have happened." Then he looked at her. "Michelle, meet Yankee." He paused for a moment. "An old colleague of sorts."

She turned slowly, looking the stranger up and down. His gun was holstered at his side now, and he looked somewhat less scary than earlier. But only just somewhat. "Mr. Yankee."

The guy chuckled. "Not mister, just Yankee. You know, like Bono."

Michelle nodded, then glanced over her shoulder at Nick. "You gonna tell me what all this was about?"

"Later. We've gotta get out of here first." He motioned to Yankee. "Lead the way."

Nick made a motion to follow the guy, but Michelle grabbed his arm. "You're forgetting something."

"I told you, I'll fill you in later."

"That's not what I'm talking about." She sighed. "But if I don't text Smith a recording soon, he'll know something went down, and he'll be looking for me. I've gotta disappear right now, or he'll get me."

Nick froze.

"She's right," Yankee said, turning back to them.

The two men exchanged a look, then they both started grinning.

"Well, then let's give this Smith dude something to keep him busy," Nick said.

"Always wanted to do a little acting," Yankee replied. "You want me to do an accent? I can do Colombian real well."

Nick rolled his eyes, while Yankee pulled Michelle's cell phone from his pocket and navigated through the menu.

Michelle leaned into Nick, bringing her mouth to his ear. "Can you trust him? He was pointing a gun at your head earlier."

"Just as I was pointing a gun at yours. Yet you trust me."

"I didn't say that."

He moved his head back to lock eyes with her. "But you do." He tipped his chin in Yankee's direction. "I trust him about as much as you trust me right now. That'll have to do."

"Hey, if you lovebirds would stop doing whatever you're doing, we could get this show on the road."

Michelle stepped away from Nick abruptly, feeling herself blush in the dark. They weren't lovebirds, far from it. They were… Well, she didn't really know what they were. No word came to mind.

"I'm ready," Nick announced and walked up to Yankee.

# 18

Yankee opened the sliding side door of a dark van. "Hop on in."

Nick got inside and offered his hand to Michelle to help her up.

Yankee hopped in and pulled the door shut behind him. He sat down on the bench opposite Nick and Michelle's. "Okay, Fox, let's talk."

Michelle stared at Yankee. "Fox? Who's Fox?"

"He is," Yankee said, pointing an Nick.

Michelle glared at Nick. "Your name is not Nick Young?"

"I'll explain later." Right now there were more important things to discuss.

Yankee should his head. "So she doesn't even know your code name? I thought she's your girlfriend. Does that mean she knows nothing about your premonitions either?"

"Premonitions?" Michelle echoed.

Nick sighed. "Thanks a lot, Yankee. Way to break the news." He squeezed her hand in reassurance, but this wasn't the time to go into long explanations about his special gift.

"You have premonitions?" she asked again.

Nick nodded. "I'm not the only one. Yankee has them too."

Yankee nodded. "Yeah. But one of them, I've been getting over and over. The premonition the inferno, the destruction, my skin melting from the intense heat."

Nick's jaw tightened. "You're actually at the explosion site when it happens? I'm not."

"What?" Yankee asked.

"I'm somewhere at a lake, on a porch of some fancy mansion."

"Tell me more," Yankee insisted.

"I'm in front of my computer. Somebody I can't see gives me iced tea to drink. I think it's poisoned, because as soon as I drink it and try to type something into the computer, my hands are paralyzed. I can't do it. I can't stop it. I'm helpless. On the screen, I can see the explosion. Then the shockwave hits the lake and catapults five sailboats right out of the water, turns them into matchsticks. It's all I see before I get slammed against the side of the house."

"Sailboats on a lake? Wonder whether that means anything..." Yankee mused, rubbing his chin. "Could be a location. And the person who gives you that iced tea that paralyzes you? Can you remember anything about him? Or her?"

Nick shook his head. "I only see a hand. It's a man, I can tell that much."

"Any rings, scars?"

"I don't remember any."

"Next time you have the premonition, focus in on that. We need to find out who's behind this. In my visions I don't see any man. You might be the first one who's gotten a glimpse of our enemy."

"Next time?" Michelle interrupted, her gaze bouncing back and forth between the two of them. "You guys are psychic?"

Yankee cleared his throat. "Something like that. But let's not get sidetracked here. Since it's pretty clear that we're seeing the same thing, it's important that we get Stargate back together. Not only are our enemies trying to pick us off one-by-one, they're also planning something major. We have to prevent it. Problem is we don't know the others or where they're hiding." He motioned to Nick. "I was lucky to find you."

"I've been working on a solution for that for a while."

Yankee slid forward on the bench opposite Nick's. "What solution?"

"Sheppard kept a private file on all his Stargate members. Names, pictures, backgrounds. Separate from the CIA's classified personnel file—which I have the feeling has been destroyed by our enemy already."

"And Sheppard's file? You think it still exists? Wouldn't whoever killed him have destroyed that one, too?"

"I don't think so. I was able to figure out that Sheppard used a second login at the CIA. The only thing is, I can't find it."

"I don't get it."

"It's not easy to explain, but I've found digital fingerprints of somebody accessing certain files, but I can't trace who. In the end it always loops back to Sheppard's old login, and that's been disabled long ago."

"A ghost login," Michelle said.

Nick whirled his head to her. "You know what I mean?"

She nodded eagerly. "I've heard of something like it." She looked at Yankee. "I was a hacker. Anyway, I've heard of ghost logins being set up by members of Anonymous to mirror a real login. But when somebody comes across it and tries to trace it, it always leads back to the real login, the one the person was shadowing or mirroring. It's impossible to trace or find. It's not hackable." She locked eyes with Nick. "Was that what you were looking for when you hacked into those servers?"

He nodded. "I was trying to get into the system administrator's logs to search for the login."

"If it's a ghost login, that wouldn't have helped you. It's not in the logs."

"Shit!" Nick shoved a hand through his hair and tossed a regretful look at his fellow Stargate agent. "Then I have no way of getting at Sheppard's files either. Sorry. That's a dead end."

"You say it's a login, right?" Yankee asked.

Nick nodded. "Yeah."

"Before Echo died, he gave me a bracelet for safekeeping. Hidden inside it, I found two strings of names and numbers, all jumbled up. I couldn't figure out what it was, but he said to find you, Fox, because you would know what to do with it." Yankee reached into his back pocket, pulled out his wallet and removed a strip of paper from it. He handed it to Nick. "That's it."

Nick looked at it. Michelle reached for his hand and pulled the piece of paper closer to her face. Nick exchanged a look with her. "What do you think?"

"It's got the right length. All logins have a minimum of ten digits. Same with the passwords."

"Can we give it a try?" Yankee asked, sounding hopeful now.

"We sure can," Nick said, bracing one hand on his thigh. "Only thing is, if this is the ghost login, then the only place it will work from is from inside CIA headquarters." He'd known all along that once he found Sheppard's second login, he would have to get into Langley to execute the rest of his plan behind the CIA's firewalls.

"Are you telling us that we need to break into Langley?"

"I wouldn't call it breaking in…"

Yankee tilted his head, giving him a doubtful look. "What would you call it then? A suicide mission?"

"It won't be a suicide mission," Nick assured him. "I have a way in. I've got Sheppard's access card."

Yankee's eyes widened. "What?"

"Well, not his actual card, but all the data that I can imprint onto a blank card to get me into Langley."

"That's stupid," Yankee interrupted. "And I'll tell you why: the CIA would have deactivated Sheppard's access after his death."

Nick grinned. "Yeah, they would have, but they couldn't, because miraculously, right after Sheppard's murder, somebody moved his access credentials to a hidden archive."

Yankee's chin dropped. "You?"

"Yours truly. Without the system administrators knowing where the data was stored, they couldn't deactivate it. Sheppard's access card is still there. And only I know where the credentials are hidden. All I need to do is hack in, pull down the data, alter it, and transfer it to a new card. Simple as that."

"When you say alter it, what exactly do you mean by that?" Yankee asked curiously.

Nick motioned to his face. "I'm gonna have to replace Sheppard's photo on file with mine."

Yankee scratched his neck. "And you're sure you can hack into their servers?"

Nick looked at Michelle who sat next to him in stunned silence. "Considering the one person who would have been able to stop me is now on our side, I don't see a problem." He squeezed her hand. "Right?"

"Piece of cake," Michelle confirmed and looked at the other Stargate agent. "Besides, I'll give him a hand."

"Well, then, I guess we only have to discuss what you'll do once you're inside Langley. What do you need me to do?" Yankee asked. "I'm afraid I'm not a computer expert, but I can have your back." He put his hand on his gun, stroking it.

"I'm afraid your little friend there will have to stay home for this mission," Nick said, grinning. "But you can do something else for me. You can be my eyes and ears while I'm inside."

Nick exchanged a look with Michelle, who nodded instantly, understanding what he meant.

"I can tap into the infrared security system so we can watch any movements," Michelle confirmed.

Nick nodded. "Let's set it up."

# 19

It took them several hours to organize everything, then, finally, after what seemed like an eternity, Yankee stopped the van in front of a run-down apartment building and looked over his shoulder.

"Get some rest. It's going to be a tough day tomorrow."

Nick nodded and reached for Michelle's hand. She rose from her seat and allowed him to help her out of the van, before slamming the door shut and heading for the apartment building.

Michelle was silent when he unlocked the building door, then led her up to his apartment and ushered her in. She watched him as he flipped the deadbolt and set the chain.

She waited for him in the middle of the living room, arms crossed over her chest. She wanted answers, and truth be told, she was surprised that she'd waited so long. Well, maybe the fact that Yankee had looked a little menacing had contributed to her artificial patience. Or maybe it had taken her a little longer to get over the shock of having had a gun pointed at her head and being locked up in a shed, before she could wrap her brain around what was going on.

Nick glanced at her from under his dark lashes, casting her an assessing look. "How are you doing?"

"Well, let's see. Considering you threatened to kill me tonight and your new friend is a little overeager with his weapon, and the fact that you two seem to be in some deep shit with the

CIA, not to mention that whole weird stuff about being psychic, I'm doing rather splendidly, I think."

Nick took a few steps toward her, sighing. "I'm sorry, Michelle, but what happened tonight wasn't something I was planning."

"I can see that. What you were planning was to use me."

He nodded, didn't even refute her claim. "I did. But like I told you already tonight, sleeping with you wasn't part of that plan." He stretched his hand out and brushed his knuckles over her cheek.

She let it happen, the touch having an oddly calming effect on her. "I know you explained. It's just a little hard to believe, particularly since it looks like there's so much at stake for you and your friend." Too much to really be concerned about the feelings of a woman. "So you were CIA? I'm sure they taught you not to let your feelings get in the way of a mission."

"They tried. But there are times in the life of a man when he has to make his own decisions. And making love to you wasn't part of my mission." He looked down at his feet. "But I understand if you don't want to believe that. You don't know me."

Surprised by his quiet demeanor, she sighed. "No, I don't know you. I don't know what's going on. You said you'd explain everything. So explain. What is this? Your talk about visions, is that all just a smokescreen?"

He lifted his head. "I wish. But it's very real. For all of us. For all of Stargate. It changed our lives. It connects us. But it also makes us a target."

"I want to understand," she said softly. "I *need* to understand."

"I promised to tell you, so I will." He took her hand and motioned to the sectional that filled half the room.

She followed him to it and sat down next to him.

"What I'm telling you, you can never tell anybody else. Anybody with knowledge about this is a threat to our enemies as well as to us."

Michelle nodded quickly. "I wouldn't know who to tell. I'm on my own." And she certainly wouldn't want to draw any attention to herself by telling fantastic stories. Who would believe her anyway?

"My special skill… I think of it as a genetic defect. To my knowledge nobody from my family has it. At least nobody ever told me about it. Not that I'm close to any of them these days. My parents are divorced, and I guess neither my father nor my mother wanted to be reminded of the mistake their marriage had been. I think they were both relieved when my visits became less frequent, and they were able to concentrate on their new families."

"That's a shame," Michelle threw in.

Nick shrugged as if he didn't care. "It is what it is. I already had a new family, one that understood me better. I was already with the CIA when Henry Sheppard recruited me. At first I thought it was for my IT abilities, which was the field I was in at Langley, but then I realized he knew that I had ESP. He'd already started a top secret program within the CIA, hiring others like me, training them. We were unique. But Sheppard understood us. He knew what it was like to be born with a special ability that you couldn't switch off. That would sometimes haunt you."

"The visions?"

"They would come out of the blue. Like a movie playing in front of your mental eye. So real that you thought it was happening right in front of you." He met her gaze then. "I saw you. The day you took me back to your apartment."

"You saw me?"

"You crossed the street without looking to the left. The taxi hit you. It flung you over its roof and tossed you on the asphalt behind it. You didn't move." He sought her eyes. "You didn't make it, Michelle."

Her breath caught in her throat, panic rising with it. "No!" She slapped her hand over her mouth.

Nick reached for her hands, pulled them into his lap, his thumbs stroking the back of them. "That's why I ran to catch you before you could cross the street. That's why I was there."

"You saw me die?" Her voice was a whisper.

He released her hands and cupped her face. "I couldn't let it happen. And when you invited me to your place to take care of my bruises, I knew I couldn't leave without making love to you. I know I should have just thanked you for the icepack and left, but knowing what had nearly happened made it impossible for me to keep my cool. I needed to feel you."

Tears stung in her eyes. "You really saved my life…" She sniffled. "But then why did you almost kill me tonight?"

He closed his eyes for a short moment. "I thought you'd been sent to kill me. Michelle, the Stargate agents are hunted. Somebody killed our leader three years ago, and the rest of us have been on the run ever since. Somebody is after us and will kill us first chance he gets. Whoever it is wants to wipe us out. We're a threat to him. And I think I know now why: he's planning something big."

"That premonition, the one with the inferno," Michelle murmured.

"Yes. It's an event in the future. And only Stargate agents know it'll happen. If we can figure out what it is, we might be able to prevent it. And I think the person who killed Sheppard knows that. That's why he needs us all dead." He brushed a hand through her hair. "When you showed up at the meet tonight, I thought you were one of his hired assassins. I'd guessed already you were working for him. I just wasn't sure whether your expertise went beyond computing."

"So you think Smith is the man who killed Sheppard?"

"Absent of any other leads, I have to assume it. At the very least, he's connected to whoever wants us dead. He got you to try to keep me out of the CIA's servers. He knows I'm trying to get at files so I can resurrect Stargate. That's why he used you to deny me access. But I have to get at those files. With them we have a better chance of finding the others."

"Don't you think he's using those same files to find all of you?"

"He probably is. We have to be faster, or he'll pick us off one-by-one."

Michelle shivered. "We can't let that happen."

He smiled suddenly. "We?"

"Well, we're a team now, aren't we? Or are you planning on pointing your gun at me again?"

He chuckled softly. "Not that kind of gun."

Michelle sucked in a breath of air, releasing it on an outraged huff. "Oh my God, I can't believe you just said that. What is it with men? Is there ever a time when you're not thinking of sex?"

Nick winked at her. "I'll let you know as soon as that happens."

# 20

Before Michelle could throw something at him, Nick pulled her into his arms and immobilized her.

"I can't help myself with you," he confessed. "I'm not normally so aggressive when it comes to women. I'm more the shy kind of guy from—"

"Yeah, yeah, from Indiana," she interrupted, rolling her eyes. "How about you drop the act and show me who you really are? Don't I deserve that after you nearly shot me tonight?"

"I didn't nearly shoot you."

"Pointing a gun at my forehead says otherwise."

"I'm never gonna live that one down, am I?"

"Not as long as I can use it as a bargaining chip," she admitted.

"I give in. What do you want?"

She lifted her chin. "You. The real you. Just for tonight. I want you to show me what's behind that façade."

"You might be disappointed. The man behind the secret agent isn't all that interesting. Just a normal guy with a not-so-normal gift. That's all."

Michelle smiled a knowing smile. "Maybe that's what I find interesting: a normal guy. My life is crazy enough. I just want to pretend for one night that I have a normal life with a normal guy and forget that the government is after both of us."

"Just for one night?"

"That's all I need."

He looked deep into her eyes, searching their blue depths for more. Was it really only one night she wanted? And what did he want? Would he be satisfied with just one, knowing that hoping for more was foolish?

"And after that?" he found himself asking.

She looked to the side, avoiding his gaze. He didn't force her head back, didn't make her tell him what she really wanted, because he knew instinctively that he couldn't give her more. "Let's not think of tomorrow."

"All right, then." He lifted her into his arms and stood. "Let's go to bed."

She laced her hands behind his neck as he carried her to his bedroom. Nick flipped the light switch on his way in, and the bedside lamps went on, bathing the room in a soft glow.

"Sorry about the mess. I don't generally have visitors."

He set her on her feet.

"I don't care. I just hope you have condoms here."

He motioned to the bedside table. "Plenty. You won't have to worry about that." He caught a curl of her hair and wrapped it around his index finger. "You should worry about how sore you'll be in the morning."

Michelle pulled his head to her face. "Don't make promises you can't keep."

"Is that a challenge?"

"What if it is?"

"Then I'm afraid *Normal Guy* here will have to draw upon his secret agent skills and show you that making fun of him is only gonna get you in trouble."

She pouted. "But I already *am* in trouble."

"Oh, this is a very different kind of trouble." He reached for her long-sleeved T-shirt and pulled it over her head. "It's the kind of trouble that is best enjoyed naked."

Her jeans landed on the floor a moment later, together with her shoes and socks. She looked utterly sexy in her black bra and matching thong.

"Does the rule about nudity apply to you, too?" she murmured.

Nick already tore at his shirt, ridding himself of it. The rest of his clothing joined his shirt only seconds later, until he stood in front of her in the nude. He'd never been shy about his body, but the way Michelle ran her eyes over him now made him more aware of it than he'd ever been before. Her gaze traveled over him until it stopped at his groin.

He took his fully erect cock into the palm of his hand and squeezed it, before stroking from tip to root. When she licked her lips, Nick involuntarily groaned, his eyes focused on those lush lips.

Her gaze shot to his face.

"Strip for me," he demanded, his voice hoarse from the arousal taking over his body. When Michelle reached behind her back, he stopped her. "Take your time with it. I like watching."

She smiled sinfully. "So that's the real Nick. Not the shy boy from Indiana, but the insatiable voyeur."

"Nothing wrong with a little voyeurism in the right place." He tilted his chin in her direction. "I loved watching you in the mirror when I took you last night. Call that voyeurism if you like. Either way—" He pointed to her bra. "—strip, baby, or I might just have to bend you over that sink again to get my kicks."

Nick noticed the visible shiver that raced over her body and the goose bumps it left in its wake. He couldn't help but smile. Yes, Michelle had thoroughly enjoyed their little interlude in the bathroom. Just thinking of it now ratcheted his own arousal higher, adding more girth to his already hard cock.

Finally, Michelle complied with his demand and slid both hands up her torso, slowly stroking her breasts. She looped her fingers under the straps of her bra and nudged them off her shoulders. The silky fabric covering her peaks started to slide, but caught on her hard nipples and prevented a further disrobing. With a coquettish look Michelle ran her fingers to her breasts and underneath the thin cups, pushing them down farther. Now her nipples were covered by her hands.

Nick gave his cock a hard tug. "Squeeze them."

Like a good girl, she did. Then she took her nipples between thumb and forefinger and rolled them.

At the erotic sight, a groan burst from him, and a drop of moisture leaked from his shaft. "Take it off," he growled.

Slowly she moved her hands behind her back to work the clasp. The action thrust her breasts toward him as if she was offering them to him. He was unable to resist and crossed the distance between them with one step.

His hands were on her breasts the moment the bra fell to the floor. They felt warm and firm in his hands. He squeezed them, gently at first, but the feel of her delectable flesh in his palms was too much to bear. He dipped his head and licked first over one then the other peak.

"How about my panties?" she asked, an air of innocence in her voice.

"I'll take care of those."

His lips around one hard peak, sucking as much of her breast into his mouth as he could, he slid his right hand down the front of her torso, until his fingers bumped against the lace waistband of her thong. Without stopping, he dipped below it, reacquainting himself with her bare sex.

With his left hand, he grabbed her leg and lifted it up to hold against his outer thigh. Michelle's arms came around him to hold on for balance, while his fingers were already busy diving deeper. Her cleft was moist and warm. Juices slicked his fingers and the scent started to permeate his bedroom. He lifted his head from her breasts.

"Aren't you a naughty girl? Look how wet you are already, and I haven't even started yet."

With heavy-lidded eyes she looked at him "Then you'd better start."

"Yeah, I'd better." He set her leg down again, then used both his hands to strip her of her panties. "Lie down on the bed."

Not taking her eyes off him, she stepped back and lowered herself onto the duvet with catlike grace. She angled one leg to give him a view of her most intimate place, as if he needed that obvious an invitation.

Nick followed her onto the bed, pushing her legs farther apart to make a space for himself. "Did you enjoy when I licked you the other day?"

Her eyes widened and a blush rose to her cheeks. "You know I did."

"Then maybe we should start with that," he proposed, dipped his head to her sex and pressed his lips to her warm and moist flesh. With his tongue, he parted her folds and lapped up her arousal.

Beneath him, Michelle trembled, making pride swell in his chest to know that he could give her this kind of pleasure. He wanted her to forget the fear of the last few hours and show her that he didn't only bring danger and menace into her life, but that he could deliver passion and pleasure as well.

When she put a hand on the back of his head and caressed his scalp, a shudder traveled through his body, sending a flame of hot desire into his groin. He moaned into her flesh, letting her know how she affected him, how her touch aroused him and her taste made him want more.

"Oh Nick," she murmured on a breathy exhale, her hips undulating.

Her words and actions spurred him on, made him lick her with even more purpose. Every moan she released, every movement of her body added to his excitement of pleasuring the beautiful woman in his arms, in his bed. Because she trusted him now, trusted him with her body, and maybe, some day, she could trust him with her heart, too. But he knew he had to earn this trust.

A change in Michelle's breathing told him that she was on the verge of her climax. A fierce sensation of possessiveness charged through him at the knowledge that he was the one to drive her to such heights. And the thought that there might be other men after him made him growl, even though he had no right to think that way. There was nothing he could offer Michelle; nothing but a life on the run.

Michelle twisted in the sheets, her moans now more pronounced, her hands fisting the duvet, knuckles white as if holding on for dear life.

He wrapped his lips around her clit and sucked the little nub into his mouth, pressing down on it, while he teased her folds with his wet finger.

Her body exploded on a moan, and he drove his finger into her spasming channel, feeling her muscles clamp down on him, imprisoning him in her warmth. Wave after wave wracked her body, her orgasm taking her, while he continued to lick over her clit, wringing more pleasure from her body.

When she collapsed with a contented sigh, Nick lifted his head.

Michelle was a sight to behold. Her face was flushed, her body glistening, nipples hard and tempting as hell. Her eyes were half-closed, but she looked at him, a soft smile playing at her plump lips.

Without a word, he leaned toward the bedside table and retrieved a condom from there. He rolled it over his aching cock and positioned himself between her spread thighs once more.

Locking eyes with her, he guided his erection to her wet sex, nudging her nether lips apart gently. In slow motion, he slid into her, feeling how the walls of her channel enveloped him in a loving caress.

Michelle's legs lifted and she wrapped them around the back of his thighs, pulling him to her. "That's good," she murmured.

"Yes." And he could make it even better, not by taking her hard and fast, but by taking his time tonight. By loving her slowly and tenderly. As if they had all the time in the world.

He braced himself on his elbows and knees, making sure not to crush her under his weight, and brushed a strand of her hair from her face. Slowly he pulled his hips back, allowing his cock to slip from her until only the tip was still inside, before descending again on a measured exhale.

"I want to make love to you all night." He brushed his lips on hers, letting her taste herself, and caressed her face with the pads of his fingers. "I want you to know that I would never hurt you."

Her lashes fluttered and she looked into his eyes. "I know that now."

"No matter what happens tomorrow, I want you to remember tonight. I want you to know that if I could, I'd give you so much more than just one night."

She opened her mouth to protest, but he put a finger across her lips.

"You deserve so much more."

He took her lips and kissed her, putting all those things he couldn't say into it, while his hips moved in an easy rhythm, his cock sliding in and out of her, unrushed, unhurried. Because tonight wasn't about the race to release, it was about the journey, about the pleasure of getting there. It was about Michelle.

His body heated and sweat built on his skin. It made the contact of skin-on-skin even smoother, even more natural and sensual.

The warmth in Michelle's eyes as she gazed at him filled his heart with hope. Her hands were on him, touching him, exploring him, caressing him. His entire body hummed with awareness, pleasure building inside him, making his heart beat faster and blood race through his veins as fast as a locomotive.

Though he didn't want to climax yet, his body didn't give him a choice in the matter. Being connected to Michelle in such an intimate way, he hurtled toward the inevitable. He couldn't have stopped it anymore than he could stop a tsunami.

When the first bolt of pleasure charged into his cock, he tried to hold it back, but the wave was already cresting, already hitting him broadside. Hot semen exploded from the tip of his cock, and spasms rocked his body, making his hips jerk and his cock slam into Michelle's soft center with such force that he feared he was going to hurt her.

But when their eyes locked, all he saw was pleasure in those blue orbs. Then her body stilled for a split second, before a visible shiver overtook her and her interior muscles gripped him tightly.

Her cry of release went through him, reigniting him, sending another intense wave of pleasure over him.

Breathing hard, he collapsed on top of her, managing only in the last second to brace himself on his elbows. His knees were shaking. Noticing Michelle's heaving chest, he rolled onto his back, releasing her.

He turned his head to the side, looking at her, unable to say a word. She shifted, facing him. He reached for her, intertwining his fingers with hers.

Wordlessly, she stared at their joined hands. He knew then that letting her go would be the hardest thing he'd ever done.

# 21

"You clean up pretty nice," Michelle said, pointing to Nick's navy business suit.

They were standing by the side of a road only two miles away from the CIA's headquarters in Langley, Virginia. They'd arrived with three cars: the van Yankee had been driving, an inconspicuous Toyota Corolla, and a gray Buick. At first Michelle hadn't understood the need for so many cars, but Yankee had explained that Nick needed to drive himself to the parking lot, since he was the only one who could get a car through the gate with his CIA identification. She and Yankee would have to wait at a safe distance. Once Nick was back, he'd have to ditch the car he'd used to get into the CIA, and they needed to be able to switch cars, in case they were being followed. Hence the need for the Buick.

Nick tugged on his tie. "Dress code is pretty formal inside Langley. I don't wanna stick out like a sore thumb."

"Don't worry, you'll fit right in," Yankee said confidently.

Michelle must have looked worried, because Nick took her hand, and squeezed it reassuringly. "I've been in there many times. I know my way around."

"What if you're recognized?" she asked.

"Even if I am, there are so many covert agents swarming around that place that nobody will ask me any questions. That's just how it is in there. Isn't that right, Yankee?"

# Fox in plain Sight 127

The other Stargate agent nodded with a grunt. "Sure is. Though it's not without risk." He motioned to the ID Nick had pinned to his breast pocket. "That'll get you in, sure, but you know as well as I do that the code embedded in Sheppard's ID will throw up all kinds of red flags. And once those work their way to the right person, the jig is up."

Michelle felt as if somebody had just choked the air out of her. "What?" She glared at Nick. "Why didn't you tell me about that? I thought nobody knew about the ID."

"That was the case while it was hidden in the secret archive, but the moment I activated it for myself, it became visible to anybody who cares to look." He shrugged. "Don't worry, this is a bureaucracy like any other. The system security administrators working for the CIA are just as overworked and underpaid as anybody else. They don't have time to chase every single abnormality."

She didn't believe him. The way he avoided her gaze now told her that he was aware of it, too.

"I've got at least an hour before they figure out the ID is bogus," Nick tried to placate her.

"At most," Yankee threw in.

Nick tossed him a sideways glance. "Not helping."

"If you're talking about backing you up when you're lying to your girlfriend about the risk you're taking, then, no, I'm not helping. I wasn't aware that was part of my job."

Michelle leaned closer to Nick. "I thought after last night…" She hesitated, searching Nick's gaze. "I thought we were gonna be honest with each other."

He brushed his knuckles over her cheek. "We are. But I didn't want to worry you. Trust me, I can do this. I worked as an IT analyst in Langley for many years. I know how things work there."

"You didn't mention that before," Yankee interrupted.

Nick shrugged. "How do you think I was able to hide Sheppard's ID in the first place? The moment I got his distress call, I did what I could to leave a back door open for myself. I knew that one day I would need to be able to get back in. But I had to run, just like the rest of you. It was all I could do in the few minutes I had." He looked back at Michelle. "I'll be in and out in no time. They won't even blink."

Despite his reassuring explanation, the doubt inside her didn't subside. "Are you sure?"

"Positive. Now—"

The pinging of Michelle's burner phone interrupted him.

She pulled it from her pocket, her heart beating in her throat. Only one person knew this number and would contact her on it: Mr. Smith.

Before she could read the text message, Nick took the cell from her and looked at it. When he looked up again, concern spread over his face, making worry lines appear on his forehead and around his eyes and mouth.

"Fucking bad timing," Nick ground out and exchanged a look with Yankee.

Michelle took the phone from him and read the message. *Now* Smith wanted a meeting? Damn it. "In two hours? That won't give us any time to set a trap for him." She looked at Nick. "We have to leave now. You have to go into Langley another day."

Nick shook his head. "I can't. The ID is already active. Tomorrow, hell, this afternoon, it will already have been flagged as bogus and they'll arrest me the moment I set foot in the building. It has to be now or never."

"Crap, crap, crap!" Michelle cursed. There was only one solution then. And as much as she hated it, she knew it was their only chance. "We have to split up."

"Out of the fucking question!" Nick bellowed.

"Just hear me out."

"Michelle, you're not meeting him alone. That's suicide."

"I have no intention of meeting him alone. But somebody has to go there to set up surveillance." She pointed to the text message. "He wants to meet on the island that houses Lady Bird Johnson Park. I know it. It's across from the Pentagon, separated by Boundary Channel."

"Boundary Channel?" Yankee asked.

"A waterway that connects to the Potomac," she explained and looked back at Nick. "There are two ways to get on and off the island: via George Washington Memorial Parkway or with a boat. There's a marina on the southern tip of the island, Columbia Island Marina."

"What are you saying?" Nick asked.

"Somebody has to set up electronic surveillance there in case he slips through our fingers. We have to be able to track whether he leaves the island by car or by boat. And I'm the only one who has the technical knowledge to do that."

"So does Yankee," Nick protested, looking at Yankee for support.

"That's right. I know my stuff." Yankee looked insulted.

Michelle tossed him a glare. "I know my stuff better, no offense. Besides, Nick needs you here. You need to guide him once he's inside. And if something goes wrong, you'll have to get him out."

She could see Nick battling with the decision before him. "I don't like it."

She sighed. "I know. But I work fast. I'll be done long before Smith shows up. By that time, you'll have left Langley and can meet me outside Arlington and then we can surprise Smith together. It's the best solution."

Nick glanced at Yankee. His friend nodded after a few seconds.

"She's right, man. We're running out of time."

Nick took both of Michelle's hands in his. "You go there, set up the cameras and you get out. You hear me? No hanging around there. Just in and out. If you're not at the Arlington Metro in exactly one hour, I'm going to whip your butt when I catch you. Is that clear?"

She nodded, her heart racing at his impassioned statement.

"Make sure Yankee can get a hold of you while I'm in there. Do you have a cell on you?"

Michelle shook her head. "Only the burner from Smith."

Nick glanced at Yankee, who already nodded and said, "I've got some spares."

Nodding in agreement, Nick addressed her again, "Take the van. It's got all the equipment you'll need." He turned to Yankee. "I'll take the Toyota. Yankee, you'll wait in the Buick and take the communication system with you so you and I can communicate when I'm inside and you can watch my back."

When Nick turned back to her, his gaze was heated. He pulled her into his arms, kissed her fiercely, then released her just as abruptly.

# 22

Nick exhaled a sigh of relief when the guard at the gate at the entrance to the CIA campus returned his identification and lifted the gate to let him pass. He pressed his foot on the gas and accelerated the Toyota, driving down the long driveway flanked by trees and bushes.

The entire Langley campus was surrounded by a thick forest, sitting there like an island. Several massive parking lots—all above ground—surrounded the large building, or rather buildings, since CIA headquarters was really made up of three separate but interconnected buildings. Once inside any of them, a person could get to any part of it—given the right access credentials of course.

An inner courtyard was partially covered with a massive tent-like canopy, other areas were open and provided some greenery to relax within the concrete-and-glass structure.

Nick drove to the parking lot closest to the main entrance. In case something went wrong, he would need to get to his car quickly to leave the CIA campus before they locked the place down. It was still early. Many employees were only just arriving. He'd timed it that way, knowing that during busy times he had a better chance of slipping through unnoticed. In the morning, everybody was too concerned with getting their first cup of coffee and not fully awake yet.

Nick exited the car and locked it, then walked calmly toward the entrance. From the corner of his eye, he observed other men

and women doing the same. Some held paper coffee cups,
others carried briefcases. Most were dressed in suits or other
business casual clothing.

For three years, Nick had waited for this opportunity, and
now it had finally come. As if he still belonged here, he walked
through the glass doors, entering the white-and-gray marble-
and-granite entrance hall. Nothing had changed. A row of
turnstiles awaited him. Beyond them the well-known CIA seal
made of white-and-gray granite tiles was laid into the floor.

He lined up at one of the turnstiles, waiting his turn to swipe
his identification card. The person ahead of him marched
through it quickly, and he followed, swiping his card.

A high-pitched beep sounded, and a red light flashed at his
turnstile.

Adrenaline shot through him.

*Shit!*

A security guard walked up to him, glancing at his ID.
"Sorry, sir, we've been having some problems with this one this
morning when people come through too quickly. Please try
again now."

Nick plastered a fake smile on his face and nodded. "No
problem."

Heart beating in his throat, he swiped his card again. A green
light flashed at once.

"Go ahead, sir," the security guard said, waving him through.
"It's all good now. Have a nice day."

"You, too."

Relieved, Nick marched through the turnstile and walked to
the end of the hall. Sweat trickled from his neck and disappeared
beneath the collar of his starched dress shirt. Another incident
like that, and he'd have a heart attack at thirty-three.

Focusing on the task ahead, Nick let his gaze roam. He still knew his way around, though it had been over three years since he'd last been at Langley. The maze of corridors had never seemed daunting to him before. He'd loved the challenge, loved to figure out the fastest way from point A to point B. Acting as if he belonged there, Nick walked confidently. He never hesitated, always planned ahead, his mind constantly mapping out the path in front of him, so he would never have to stop to orient himself. He wouldn't give anybody a reason to look at him with suspicion.

He didn't take the elevator, but used the stairs instead, not wanting to be in a confined space from which it would be difficult to escape should anybody recognize him. Though it was unlikely, there was always a chance of running into somebody who knew Sheppard and therefore knew the badge that hung on Nick's pocket wasn't his, even though the picture was of his face.

It felt like an eternity until he reached the right corridor. He approached the door that said *Restricted Area* and stopped. Outside of it were a card reader and a camera.

Nick swiped his card, then lifted his face toward the camera, knowing that a facial recognition software was about to scan his face and compare it to the picture on file—the picture he'd uploaded to the CIA's systems himself.

Several seconds passed, then he heard a click. Nick pushed against the door. It opened inward. He stepped through it and let the door close behind him. It was quieter here, though he knew he wasn't alone. Along the corridor were several rooms with their doors closed.

"I'm in," he whispered into the tiny mic hidden beneath the lapel of his jacket.

"Good, I've got you."

He heard Yankee's reply in his ear and sighed with relief. The GPS in the heel of Nick's shoe was sending back a signal to his fellow Stargate agent. The infrared system Michelle had tapped into and showed Yankee how to use, was doing the rest.

"Walk straight ahead," came the first instruction through his earpiece.

With an outward calmness, Nick passed the closed doors until he reached a bend in the corridor.

"Now left."

He turned left.

"Third door."

Nick counted. At the third door, he stopped. There was only a number on it, no other indication of what lay behind it.

"Is it empty?" Nick asked, keeping his voice low.

"Yes. Infrared indicates no human inside. It's a go."

Nick pushed the door open and slipped in, easing it shut behind him. The humming noise in the room was created by the many computers lining one wall.

"I'm going silent," he advised Yankee.

"Understood."

Nick walked up to the first computer and touched the mouse. The login screen came on as expected. He pulled the paper Yankee had given him from his pocket and placed it next to the keyboard, then typed in the string of numbers and letters into the login and password area on the screen. Praying he was correct that this was Sheppard's ghost login, he pressed the *Enter* key.

It only took a second for a blue desktop to appear. *Welcome, Henry,* it said in large letters before the writing faded into the background, and made way for several icons.

It wasn't hard to navigate the area. Sheppard had been an organized man, keeping everything in its proper place.

Under a folder named *Family*, Nick found a folder simply named *My Boys*. For Sheppard, his Stargate agents had been his family.

For a brief instant, Nick's heart clenched. Sheppard had truly been a father to him, and most likely to the other Stargate agents, too. To know that he had seen them as his sons, brought back the pain of losing him. But he had no time to wallow in that pain now.

Nick clicked on the folder.

Shock made him jerk back. The folder was empty.

"Shit!" he cursed.

"What's wrong?" Yankee asked.

"Not now!"

Frantically, Nick searched the remainder of the folders. Empty, all of them!

"Fuck!" he cursed. "Somebody got here ahead of us! The files are all gone!"

"Shit!" Yankee ground out.

"Wait!" He'd just had an idea. "The recycle bin." Maybe it hadn't been emptied and the deleted files were still sitting in there.

Nick clicked on the icon. Empty, too.

"Fuck!" All this for nothing. He kicked against the desk, frustrated. "Somebody knew we'd be coming."

"Get out of there!" Yankee ordered. "Now!"

"There must be another way," Nick mumbled to himself. There had to be. He scanned all icons on the desktop once more.

"Damn it, Fox, you've gotta leave!"

Nick shook his head, when his eyes suddenly fell on an icon he'd ignored. "The backup system."

"What?"

"All computers are backed up regularly. The backup files are kept for quite some time." He only had to figure out where the backup files were kept.

Quickly, Nick opened the control panel and searched for the right area then scanned the information and found the file path he was looking for.

Moments later, he'd navigated to it. There were hundreds of backup files pertaining to Sheppard's files. They were listed chronologically. The last one had been made about a month after Sheppard's death. Since then, the files in his cloud hadn't been backed up, most likely because the system hadn't detected any activity.

Nick opened the last backup file, the one made after Sheppard's death, but no folder with the name *My Boys* was among it. This meant that somebody had erased it within a month after the Stargate program's leader had been murdered.

Remembering Sheppard's date of death all too well, Nick clicked on the file with a date only two days prior.

"Shit, Fox!" Yankee's voice came through his earpiece. "Somebody's coming. You've gotta hightail it outta there."

"I only need a minute," he said, already perusing the contents of the backup file. "There! Got it!" The folder named *My Boys* was right there. Nick clicked on it, and a long list of individual files appeared, all carrying only initials.

Nick pulled a flash drive from his pocket, jammed it in the computer's USB port. Immediately, an alert flashed on the screen: *Copying disabled.* He'd expected this, but thanks to his years in the CIA's Data Security department, he knew a way around it. He typed in the appropriate command and seconds later, copied the entire folder. A window popped up, indicating the number of megabytes it was copying and the time left.

"Damn it, Fox! Get your ass out of there now!"

"Almost there, just twenty more seconds!"

Drumming his fingers on the desk, he watched the time on the window decrease. "Ten seconds."

"Now, Fox, now!"

The window closed, indicating that the copying process was complete. Nick pulled the flash drive from the USB port and shut the computer down.

He headed for the door.

"Fuck!" he cursed and whirled back around. "The login credentials."

"Leave 'em!" Yankee ordered.

"Can't!" He rushed back to the computer, snatched the piece of paper from the desk and ran back to the door. He eased it open.

"Turn right! Into the office next to you."

Nick followed Yankee's command without hesitation and dove into the room next to the one he'd just exited. Just in time, as it turned out. Footsteps passed by his door. Then the door to the other room was opened and closed.

"Now, out!" Yankee ordered.

Breathing heavily, Nick exited the room and walked back the same way he'd come. At the door, he stopped for a brief moment, then he pushed it open and left the restricted area.

As he walked through the maze of corridors, back toward the main entrance, he glanced at one of the clocks on the wall. It was high time that he left. His hour was almost up. Shortly, a vigilant system administrator would realize that the ID Nick was using belonged to a dead man. But before that happened, Nick had to get back to the computer Yankee was using to keep tabs on him, and replace his photo on Sheppard's ID with Sheppard's original one.

He increased his speed, but didn't run. It would only draw suspicion onto him. At the next turn, he reached the entrance hall. Ahead of him was the oversized seal of the CIA, and beyond it were the turnstiles. Nick let his eyes roam. The security guard who'd assisted him earlier was gone, probably on a break. Somebody else had taken his place. Good. It meant the guy wouldn't get suspicious seeing him leave again so quickly.

Trying to appear as relaxed and calm as he could under the circumstances, Nick walked past the turnstiles and through the glass doors into the open air. He didn't look back, and continued in the same tempo until he reached the Toyota.

"I'm outside."

"Good. I'll be right there."

Nick unlocked the car and got inside. When the engine started, he felt a little better already, but only once he'd passed through the gate, leaving the CIA campus, did his heart beat normally again.

The Buick with Yankee was waiting for him in a side street about two miles from the CIA's security gate.

Nick pulled over, killed the engine, and took out a special antiseptic wipe, ripped open the package and proceeded to wipe down the steering wheel, gear stick, and anything else he'd touched. Not only would it make sure he didn't leave any fingerprints behind, it would also get rid of any DNA. He finished by wiping the outside door handle, before he stuffed the used wipe and packaging into his pocket then got into the waiting Buick.

Yankee pulled into the street the moment Nick was inside the car. "You got it?"

Nick patted his jacket pocket. "I've got it." Then he looked at his watch. "Step on the gas, Yankee. Michelle is waiting for us."

Nick reached for his computer on the back seat, jetpack already attached, and didn't lose any time wiping out any trace of his picture on Sheppard's old CIA access card.

It took them less than ten minutes on the George Washington Memorial Parkway to reach the Arlington Metro station.

Nick searched for the van. "Do you see her?"

"Nothing," Yankee said.

"Shit!" Nick cursed and looked at his watch again. Then his nape began to prickle uncomfortably. "Something isn't right. Shit, something happened to Michelle."

# 23

Michelle cursed. She'd wanted to place only one more camera, but had remembered too late that the northbound lane on George Washington Memorial Parkway didn't have an exit on Columbia Island. So she'd had to double-back after installing a camera right off the highway where the Pentagon Lagoon Yacht Basin was flowing back into the Potomac River. The bridge was a strategic point from which any boat leaving the lagoon could be watched.

Unfortunately the detour had cost her precious minutes. Minutes, it now turned out, she didn't have. Because she wasn't the only early bird.

"Well, look who couldn't wait to meet," the stranger said in a menacing voice, as he gripped her elbow.

She knew immediately that this wasn't Smith. His voice sounded different, and he let her see his face. Smith had always made sure she never got a glimpse of him so she couldn't identify him.

One thing was immediately crystal clear: this man had been sent by Smith to get rid of her.

"Let's go somewhere more private," he suggested, jamming something hard—and concealed beneath the jacket that he'd slung over his forearm—into her side.

She didn't need to see the item to know it was a gun. She also knew immediately why he wanted to head away from the path that led back to where she'd parked the van. A group of three-to-five year olds was playing in the open meadow only a few yards away, supervised by three young kindergarten teachers. He couldn't kill her here, or he would have several witnesses and a panicked group of kids on his hands.

Just as Michelle knew she couldn't call out to the three teachers for help either. It would only endanger the children. For all she knew, the man currently holding a gun to her ribs had no scruples killing innocent children in order to save his own ass.

She was on her own.

"Move!" he ordered between clenched teeth.

She cast him a sideways glance. He looked so normal. Not like a villain, but more like a boring accountant on his way to work. That's why she hadn't even noticed him, though clearly he'd noticed her.

Michelle had no choice but to put one foot in front of the other. But she had to somehow buy herself time. "Smith sent you? What does he want?"

A little chuckle came from the man. "What do you think?" He pressed the barrel of the gun harder into her side to make his point.

"Why? I've done everything he wanted."

The assassin nudged her in the direction of a public restroom, which was partially surrounded by bushes and trees.

"Apparently your employer wasn't quite satisfied with your job performance."

"I can improve," she hastened to say, realizing that once they reached the restrooms there was nothing to prevent him from killing her out of sight of any witnesses.

"I believe your probationary period is over. And guess what?" He leaned in. "You didn't make the cut."

Her heart beat frantically, and her palms were sweaty. "Whatever he's paying you, I can pay you more."

A snort was his answer. He didn't believe her. Well, she wouldn't believe herself either.

Michelle eyed the one-story brick building that housed the restrooms and saw a man exit from one side. He walked toward them.

The assassin pasted a smile on his face and said for the benefit of the man passing them, "Honey, your stomach will feel better in a second, I promise you."

The fake sweet tone of his voice made her want to puke and make his lie about her stomach trouble true.

The moment the other man was out of earshot, her assailant hurried her along. "Let's move."

She pretended to stumble over her own feet, letting out a gasp. He gripped her elbow even harder, his gun slipping for a moment, but then he pulled her along again. The distraction had worked, however: she'd managed to pull the cell phone Yankee had given her from her pocket, press what she hoped was the redial button, and drop it into the grass. Yankee had programmed in his number, and they'd tested it before she'd left with the van. She could only hope now that he would get the message that she was in trouble. It was a long shot, but what else could she do?

"Stop, please," she begged loudly, praying that the call had already connected and would pick up her voice from this distance. "My ankle. I think I sprained it. Please don't take me into those public restrooms. Please don't kill me."

"Shut up, you bitch!" he growled, looking around. He seemed satisfied that nobody was close enough to have heard her or seen her struggle.

Her gaze darted past the structure ahead of them, where sailboats and motorboats were docked at the small marina. But it was quiet there, too.

With every step they got closer to the public restrooms, hope that the cavalry would arrive in time faded a little bit more. A hand clamped around her heart and squeezed it tighter with every second. Soon, it would all be over. This wasn't how she'd imagined her end: shot in a public restroom, her body lying on the urine-stained concrete floor. A cold shiver raced down her back, and her hands trembled.

Tears welled in her eyes, and she didn't even try to blink them back. Nobody would see them, nobody but her killer.

"Please," she murmured, but he'd already opened the door to the women's restroom and shoved her inside.

A single neon light flickered on the ceiling. Except for the dripping faucet it was quiet. There were three stalls, their doors open. The smell of human waste hit her immediately, making her nose twitch uncomfortably. A morbid thought came: at least she wouldn't have to bear the stench for long.

For the first time since the assassin had caught her, he released her elbow and pushed her from him, toward one of the stalls. She whirled around, needing to watch him. As if seeing the gun would somehow help her stop him.

With a serenity only a professional killer could exhibit, he pulled a silencer from his jacket pocket. He placed the jacket over the waste bin, then slowly screwed the silencer onto the barrel of his pistol.

"It won't hurt," he promised.

"Please, just let me go. I promise I'll disappear today. Nobody has to find out that you didn't kill me. I'll leave the country."

The assassin shook his head. "Sorry, lady, but I always fulfill my duty."

Instinctively, she shrank back, stepping deeper into the stall until her legs backed up against the toilet bowl.

The cocking of the gun echoed off the walls. The sound thundered in her ears and made her heart stop. This was it then. The end.

Another sound, that of creaking door hinges, reached her ears a split second later.

Her head veered in the direction of the door as it opened. Oh, no, another innocent woman would have to die because she was about to witness a murder.

"No! Run!" Michelle screamed at the person she couldn't even see, because the assassin was blocking her view of the door.

He spun around, his back to her now, his gun hand outstretched.

The shot echoed louder than she would have expected. She'd always thought a silencer would dampen the sound of the gunshot to a dull rumble. But this was different, louder, deafening.

Paralyzed, she stared at the assassin's back, expecting him to turn around to her now and finish her. But instead, his knees buckled and he collapsed onto the dirty floor. Her gaze flew to the door. Nick stood there, a gun in his hand.

"Are you all right?" he asked, rushing toward her.

She nodded, but couldn't get a single word over her lips.

Nick sidestepped the dead body and reached for her, pulling her out of the stall. "We have to leave. Now. Before anybody sees us."

She nodded numbly and clung to his hand as he dragged her out of the bathroom and around to the other side, away from the entrance.

The van, its engine running, was waiting for them. For a moment she wondered how that was possible, since she still felt the key to it in her pocket. But Yankee probably had a second one on him.

"Hop in, quickly!" Nick demanded, helping her into the van and jumping in behind her, then slamming the door shut.

The van was already in motion, making her stumble before she was able to sit on the bench.

"Get us outta here, Yankee!" Nick sat on the bench beside her and pulled her into his arms.

His erratic breathing and heaving chest mirrored her own.

"I thought I'd be too late."

Michelle buried her head in his chest, still not being able to comprehend how she'd escaped certain death. "You came. You killed him before he could kill me."

"Shame the guy's dead. Would have loved to question him about this Smith character. Guess we blew our chance there," Yankee threw in.

"Yeah, well, I had no choice," Nick answered.

He put his hand under her chin and tipped her face up. His mouth was on hers a moment later, kissing her with a desperation she'd never felt from him before. When he released her moments later, he stroked his hand over her hair.

"You scared the shit out of me, Michelle."

"I didn't know he was gonna send an assassin. And I couldn't know he'd be an hour early." Then she looked at Yankee, who was driving fast. "Where are we going?"

Nick answered in his stead. "To a safe house."

Relieved, Michelle exhaled. "What happened at Langley? Did you get the file?"

Nick grinned and patted his jacket pocket. "We got it, baby."

# 24

After arriving at the safe house, they'd analyzed the files Nick had copied, which turned out to be a veritable treasure trove of information. The files identified over thirty Stargate agents. Mostly code names, real names, and pictures were there, but the files didn't contain any mention of relatives or where the agents were from. However, there were other useful tidbits: hobbies, special skills, as well as the professions the agents had previously held. It would help Nick and his new friend in their search for the others.

Several hours after rescuing Michelle from the assassin and analyzing the files in the safe house, Nick kicked his apartment door shut with the heel of his boot and trained his eyes on Michelle who'd entered ahead of him.

She walked toward the sofa, sashaying her sweet ass for his benefit, making it hard for him to concentrate on what he had to get off his chest. When she turned and let herself sink into the cushions, resting her head against the backrest and blowing out a breath, Nick marched toward her.

His heart was still pounding out of control at the recollection of what had happened this morning. It had been close. Too damn close. And it had made him realize one thing: that he didn't want to lose Michelle. Which was why it was so hard to do what he'd promised her. To help her get away. But a promise was a promise. She'd upheld her part of the bargain, and he had to uphold his.

She smiled at him, clearly oblivious to the turmoil raging inside him. And how should she know? He hadn't told her even once what he'd started feeling.

"Something wrong?" she murmured, reaching for him.

Nick remained standing in front of her, searching for the right words. "I don't think I'm able to uphold my end of the bargain about getting you out of the country."

She shifted on the sofa. "But you promised to give me a new identity."

"I did. But I can't help you disappear." He shook his head. "Not the way you were hoping to anyway. Smith has you in his crosshairs. And knowing what I know now, that one of our own turned bad and worked for our enemies, I have to assume that Echo wasn't the only one. Smith might have other Stargate agents on their side."

"But what's that got to do with you giving me a new identity?"

"Everything. Any of those Stargate agents who've gone bad can have a premonition about you, where you are, what you're doing. If I send you away to South America on your own, you'll be without protection if one of them comes after you."

"But the chances of that happening—"

"—are real," he cut her off. And that made his blood curdle.

"But if I stay here as myself, he'll get me, too."

"If you stay here, I'll be able to watch out for you. To protect you."

*To be close to you*, he wanted to add, but didn't.

He could see how the wheels in Michelle's brain turned feverishly. Hesitantly, he said, "You'll get a new identity, but you'd be staying close... close to me."

Her eyelashes lifted, almost hitting her brows. Blue eyes stared at him with an intensity that almost knocked him off his feet.

Slowly, her lips parted, curving into a tentative smile. "So that's what this is about."

"What's what about?"

"You actually want to go out with me. You want to be my boyfriend."

"It's just so I can keep an eye on you," Nick said quickly.

Shit, he wasn't good at talking about stuff like this. He'd much rather discuss some software code with Michelle than confess what he was feeling. Besides, what if she didn't feel the same? After all, she barely knew him, he'd lied to her for half of the time they'd known each other, and he'd put her in mortal danger. Not exactly a good place to start from when applying for the position as lover and boyfriend. How was he ever going to overcome that kind of handicap?

She rose from the couch. "What exactly do you want to keep an eye on?" She unexpectedly pulled her black T-shirt over her head and tossed it on the sofa, casting him a saucy look. "My boobs?"

Nick's breath caught as he stared at her black bra. Was she going to strip in front of him?

She kicked off her shoes, then opened the button of her jeans and pulled the zipper down. "Or are you more interested in my ass and legs?"

Before she could push her jeans down, he imprisoned her hands, stopping her.

"This isn't about sex, Michelle."

She lifted her chin. "Then what is it about, Nick? What is it that you want? Because unless you tell me, I'm not gonna know what you really want."

"You're gonna make me say it, aren't you?"

She nodded slowly. "Don't I deserve that?"

He swallowed. "Oh, you deserve so much. It's just, I'm not the kind of guy who's used to talking about... well, about what he feels."

"And here, I thought you were such a smooth talker, flirting with me so I'd sleep with you."

"It's different now."

She took a step closer. "Yeah? What's different?"

"After what happened today, after almost losing you..." He shoved a hand through his hair. "...I don't think I could handle if something happened to you..." He sighed. "Damn it, Michelle, maybe you could help me a little here."

"How?"

"By telling me that I mean something to you?"

A soft smile that extended to her eyes formed on her lips. Her hand came up and she stroked his cheek. "Oh, Nick, the shy boy from Indiana. He's still in there, isn't he? And he's afraid to say what he feels because he's worried that he'll be rejected, just like his parents rejected him." She shook her head.

How could she know what was holding him back? "How do you—?"

"You told me so yourself, Nick. You told me that your parents didn't really want to see you after the divorce. I don't need to be a psychologist to guess what that would have done to that boy." She ran her finger along his lower lip. "Now try again. Give me a reason to stay."

Nick took a deep breath. "I'm in love with you. I know it's happening too fast, but if you believe in love at first sight, then believe in this. Believe that I've fallen for you and that I'll do everything in my power to protect you."

Her fingers stroked gently over his cheek. "Now, was that so hard?" She brushed her lips on his. "So does that mean I get to move in with you?"

He pulled his head back, grinning, his confidence at an all time high now. "I think you're forgetting something."

She looked at him quizzically. "What?"

"That you have to give me a reason to let you move in."

She chuckled, and her breath tickled his lips. "What if I told you that despite you lying to me at every turn, you've managed to work yourself into my heart?" She paused for a moment. "And then there's the fact that you saved my life, not once but twice. I think that needs to be rewarded."

"Rewarded, how?" He slid his arm around her waist and pulled her against him.

"You get to choose your reward."

Nick grinned from one ear to the other. "Well, in that case..." He lifted her into his arms and carried her into the bedroom.

"You're very predictable," she said, a soft laugh rolling over her lips.

"Yeah, well, I'm not really concerned about that right now." He placed her on the bed and rid himself of his suit jacket. "Get naked, baby, 'cause I'm ready for my reward."

Moments later, he joined Michelle in bed, both of them now naked.

He rolled over her, bracing himself above her. "As to your question about what I'm gonna keep an eye on most... That would be this part here." He tapped against her temple. "Just to make sure you don't come up with another brilliant idea that puts you in danger."

"I did n—"

He drowned her protest with a kiss. Like a kitten, she yielded to him immediately. He pulled back for a second. "Now about that reward..." He rolled off her then pulled her on top of him. "I don't think you've ridden me yet."

She pushed herself up, her legs sliding to either side of his hips. "Are you sure you really want to relinquish control to me?" Her eyes sparkled and her smile was sinful.

Nick felt himself grow harder beneath her core. "Michelle, when it comes to you I never had any control to begin with. So why start now?" He rocked his hips upward, nudging her with his cock. "Can't you feel what you're doing to me? This shy boy from Indiana is at your mercy."

She shook her head, laughing, and leaned toward the bedside table to snatch one of the condoms there. "Then let's put this shy boy out of his misery." With skilled hands she sheathed him, then got on her knees, adjusting her position above him.

He placed his hands on her hips. "Yes, let's," he agreed and thrust his cock upward, while pulling her down onto him at the same time.

A surprised gasp burst from her.

Nick pressed his head into the pillows, fighting against the intense pleasure that nearly sent him over the edge. Fuck! He'd never been so sensitive.

"I thought you'd given me control," she said.

He flashed her a grin. "But you *are* in control, Michelle, because you're the one guiding my body. You're the one who's making me thrust into you." To underscore his words, he lifted her hips up again, then pulled them down onto him, once more impaling her on his shaft.

Michelle grabbed his wrists and pried them from her hips, then leaned forward and pinned them to the sides of his head. Her breasts brushed his chest, sending a thrill through his body.

"I don't think you grasp the concept of giving control to somebody else. Now be good and let me teach you."

"I can't wait for that lesson to start."

The moment Michelle started to rotate her hips, grinding her sex against him, moving up and down on him, he realized that he would thoroughly enjoy this lesson. She released his wrists, and he didn't lose any time bringing his hands to her breasts. He caressed them and palmed the warm flesh, playing with her rosy nipples, turning them into hard peaks.

Like a goddess, she rode him, her movements smooth, her rhythm even, her tempo increasing with every minute. Her torso started to glisten, pearls of sweat beading on her skin, a rivulet of it soon trickling down between her breasts.

He feasted his eyes on her, drinking in her beauty, and reveling in the sensations she sent through his body. Her sex was slick and warm, her muscles tight around his erection. Her dark blond hair brushed against her shoulders with every movement, and her breasts bounced up and down, providing him with a tantalizing sight.

Unable to resist, he pulled her down to him, close enough so he could capture one nipple in his mouth and suck on the delicious bud. She moaned out loud then, and he moved to the other breast, inflicting the same treatment there, while he squeezed both breasts, kneading them.

Lower, his hips moved more urgently now, thrusting upward on each of Michelle's downward movements, slamming his cock harder into her in a quest for more friction.

Her muscles tightened around him, sending a shockwave through his body. He expelled a breath of air, and with it, his climax unexpectedly broke over him.

"Fuck!" he cursed, unable to hold back now. He looked at Michelle's face and saw how she'd thrown her head back, eyes closed, and moaned.

Then he felt her muscles spasm around him, and relief flooded him at the knowledge that she was climaxing with him.

He pulled her head down, his lips finding hers in an all-consuming kiss. He couldn't stop devouring her. Couldn't stop exploring her mouth and showing her what she meant to him, knowing that words would never be enough to express how Michelle made him feel.

Whole.

# 25

Nick hung the towel over the rack in the bathroom and pulled on his shorts, glancing back at Michelle who was stepping out of the shower, water pearling off her perfect skin.

"Damn, you look tempting," he said, letting his gaze roam over her curves.

"Haven't you had enough for today?"

He grinned, already stalking toward her, his cock thickening again. "Apparently, you've given me an endless appetite."

The ringing of the doorbell stopped him from pulling Michelle into his arms. He turned his head involuntarily.

"That'll be the Chinese I ordered," Michelle said.

He arched an eyebrow.

"Considering the calories we burned earlier, I figured we needed some food."

He grinned. "You figured right." He pressed a kiss on her cheek. "I'll go down and get it."

Nick snatched a T-shirt from the hook on the bathroom door and slipped it over his head, already walking into the hallway. He reached for his wallet and headed down the stairwell, leaving the door to his apartment ajar. The buzzer in his apartment had been broken for months, so he had no choice but to run down to the first floor.

"Coming!" he called out a few seconds before he reached the entrance door and ripped it open.

The guy standing there wore a baseball cap, kept his head down, and carried a white plastic bag with several food cartons bearing Chinese symbols. It was the food Michelle had ordered, all right, but the guy delivering it wasn't working for the Chinese restaurant around the corner. He was neither Chinese nor the kind of guy who'd take a menial job like delivering food unless it was to gain access somewhere.

The stranger lifted his face, giving Nick a full view of his features now. It was confirmation of what he already knew, what he'd already sensed by the prickling sensation spreading over his skin.

"I'm—"

"—a Stargate agent, I know," Nick cut him off, darting quick looks up and down the street to see if they were alone.

"I came alone."

"How did you find me?"

"Sheppard's ID card. When it was activated, all kinds of alarm bells went off. I got an alert. Missed you when you left Langley, but I found you again."

His pulse kicked up. "How? I covered my tracks."

"Don't worry, the only reason I was able to see your picture on Sheppard's ID was because the alert came through the moment you activated it. When I got the second alert after the system administrators disabled access, your picture was gone already." Ace winked. "Lucky for me that I took a screenshot."

Nick sighed a breath of relief.

"I hope you found what you were looking for at Langley."

"Your father was a very clever man."

The other man's eyes widened. "You recognize me?"

Nick opened the door wider, motioning him into the entrance hall. "You're Ace, Sheppard's adopted son." He offered his hand and Ace shook it. "I'm Fox. I recognize you from the picture in your father's files." Which was also the reason why he knew he could trust this man. Sheppard's son was the person who'd loved him most and would have never betrayed him.

"You found his files?" Excitement shone in Ace's eyes.

"I'm not the only one who has a copy of them though. Whoever killed your father knew about the files. He tried to delete them, probably copied them for himself first. But I was able to find a backup copy."

Ace's jaw set into a grim line. "So that's how he's been able to set those assassins on our tail. He knows who we are."

"We?"

"I'm in contact with another Stargate member, Zulu."

"You trust him?"

"One hundred percent."

"Good. We'll need him. There is another one I know: Yankee. He's in D.C. We're working on a plan to bring Stargate back together."

"That's better news than I expected," Ace admitted.

"We can do with a bit of good news, because the rest... Something bad is gonna happen." He met Ace's eyes.

"The inferno," his fellow Stargate agent said without hesitation.

"Yes. We need to find out where and when it's supposed to happen so we can prevent it," Nick said.

"It won't be easy."

Nick smiled. "We have everything we need now: a list of agents with pictures and names, and four Stargate agents working together to find them. And once Stargate rises again, we'll find the asshole who took out Sheppard and sent us running for our lives. And we'll finish this."

A slow smile built on Ace's face. "I'm glad I found you."

And for the second time in three years, Nick was glad that somebody had been able to track him down. Because having a man like Sheppard's son on their side, a man who probably knew more about the program than anybody else, was an asset they couldn't do without.

"Come on, we've got a lot to discuss."

~ ~ ~

# ABOUT THE AUTHOR

Tina Folsom was born in Germany and has been living in English speaking countries for over 25 years, since 2001 in California, where she's married to an American.

Tina has always been a bit of a globe trotter: after living in Lausanne, Switzerland, she briefly worked on a cruise ship in the Mediterranean, then lived a year in Munich, before moving to London. There, she became an accountant. But after 8 years she decided to move overseas.

In New York she studied drama at the American Academy of Dramatic Arts, then moved to Los Angeles a year later to pursue studies in screenwriting. This is also where she met her husband, who she followed to San Francisco three months after first meeting him.

In San Francisco, Tina worked as a tax accountant and even opened her own firm, then went into real estate, however, she missed writing. In 2008 she wrote her first romance and never looked back.

She's always loved vampires and decided that vampire and paranormal romance was her calling. She now has 43 novels in English and several dozens in other languages (Spanish, German, and French).

For more about Tina Folsom:
http://www.tinawritesromance.com
https://www.youtube.com/c/TinaFolsomAuthor
http://instagram.com/authortinafolsom
https://www.bookbub.com/authors/tina-folsom
http://www.facebook.com/TinaFolsomFans
You can also email her at tina@tinawritesromance.com